The Mystery of THE FILM CITY

By G. H. TEED.

No. 644 (New Series).—SEXTON BLAKE LIBRARY.
THE LEADING DETECTIVE-STORY MAGAZINE. Four New Volumes appear on the first Thursday of next month. Order them NOW!

The Mystery of The Film City
By G. H. TEED.

A wonderful novel of mystery and exciting incidents in Hollywood and Los Angeles. Featuring GEORGE MARSDEN PLUMMER, ex-Scotland Yard detective, now the most wanted criminal, with his newly acquired companion, the beautiful VALI MATA-VALI.

The Mystery of The Film City

By G. H. Teed

From *The Sexton Blake Library*
Periodical No. 644 dated 1938

Stillwoods Edition 2018

Stillwoods.Blogspot.Ca

Catalogue Information:
Title: The Mystery of The Film City
Author: G. H. Teed (George Heber Hamilton Teed (1886-1939))
Digitized from: The Sexton Blake Library, a periodical No. 644, dated 1938. Probably originally from The Sexton Blake Library, No. 119, dated 1927 and uncredited.
This Edition by: Stillwoods, 2018.
Blog: Stillwoods.Blogspot.Ca
Storefront: http://www.lulu.com/spotlight/lulubook22
ISBN Canada: 978-1-988304-50-2

Description: This is a short novel, a suspense mystery from the 1920s, with the locale of California, Hollywood. Some characters in this story have appeared in previous stories. Sexton Blake is a resident of London, U.K. Two of the villains have also appeared in this long lasting periodical and other serial publications of the time.

"Sexton Blake Library
Total Issues: 382+744+526=1652; starting September 1915.

Featuring long stories of the titular detective hero, it ran in parallel with the weekly Union Jack, and in fact long outlived that publication, lasting into the 1960s; "complete detective stories, of about 35,000 words... The same central characters - Sexton Blake, Paula Dane and Tinker - are invariably involved".

The SBL was also translated into foreign languages from the 1930s on; one edition was published in Buenos Aires as "El Neuevo Magazine Sexton Blake" in the 1940s and 1950s; other editions appeared in Norway, Sweden, Finland, Denmark, Holland, Portugal and Spain, and also translated in Hindustani."

From *philsp.com*, (links are dynamic). This website is the best one to research old magazines.

Introduction: In these Stillwoods editions we have tried to provide a bit of information about the author as in several, probably most cases, the authors are not only unknown to the reader, but they are unknown to Wikipedia and in this case The Canadian Encyclopedia. Below we provide a very early introduction:

I Meet Mrs. Teed
by W. O. G. Lofts

This article first appeared in COLLECTORS' DIGEST Vol.22 Issue 258 June 1968.

It is still remarkable when I think of it. After searching Wales for the widow of Mr. Gwyn Evans, and eventually finding her actually living a short distance away from me in London in the NW1 district, I then find the widow of Mr. G. H. Teed, after searching London, living down in South Wales. Such is the experiences of a researcher.

Now living at Penarth, a suburb of Cardiff, is an elderly lady who has very nostalgic memories about the greatest of all pre-war Sexton Blake authors. Her name of course is Mrs. Ivy Teed. Now aged 78, I have found her an extremely interesting correspondent, and with the mental abilities of one many years younger. Especially so where data is concerned about such a great author. Such was my interest in the letters that Mrs. Teed wrote me, that I thought it worth while a visit to see her. In conversation, one can get through far more things than lengthy correspondence. Accepting Mrs. Teed's kind invitation to lunch, I caught the now fast Pullman train from Paddington, and within three hours was meeting Mrs. Teed at her home, where she now lives with her sister.

Looking younger than her years; Mrs. Teed bears some resemblance to Barbara Mullen of 'Dr. Finlay's Casebook', and I soon found that she was an extremely well educated and cultured person. During our talks, I was able to gather quite a large number of new facts about George Hamilton Teed. Mrs. Teed always used to call him

'Hamilton' and so for the sake of brevity I will likewise call him that in this article.

George Heber Hamilton Teed, to give him his full correct name, was born at a small place near St. John's, New Brunswick, Canada. His father was Almon Isiah Teed, a very prosperous merchant, who owned saw-mills, a fleet of boats, a coffee plantation in South America, and also used to ferry goods right out to the West-Indies. At an early age Hamilton's father died, and his mother married again, but his father's business was shared out between him and his two sisters. Educated at Canada's most exclusive school, McGill's University, Hamilton, it could be said, had as good an education as anyone in this world. Whilst in his teens, Hamilton, who by this time had had a step-brother who he simply did not get on with at all, decided to see the world: "I wanted to see the palm trees" was his explanation many years later to Mr. H. W. Twyman, editor of the UNION JACK. Hamilton certainly saw far more than this; as he travelled round the world twice before eventually finishing up as a sheep-farmer in Australia.

Unfortunately, the drought one year beat our author, and early 1912 saw him on the boat to England almost broke, and with no prospects of a job in the home country. During the long voyage 'home' as it were, Hamilton made the acquaintance of a lady name Mrs. Storm. One only has to experience the long journey on a passenger liner to appreciate the fact that within a short time Hamilton became great friends with her. Listening sympathetically to his troubles and hard luck down-under, Mrs. Storm, who by her account had recently lost her husband and was a widow, was on the way back to England to inform his publishers of his death, and to get them to publish some of his work, which she had found amongst his (Michael Storm's) effects.

Becoming greatly interested in the scripts that Mrs. Storm showed him, eventually it was decided that Hamilton would write some stories and Mrs. Storm would take them up to Fleetway House and get them published as being by the hand of the late Michael Storm. It should be added that Michael was regarded as a brilliant author and anything from his pen was usually accepted without question. As it is well known now, this materialised, and eventually Hamilton appeared himself to the astonishment of Willie Back (the then editor of UNION JACK), who thought that the 'ghost' of Michael Storm must really have arrived, as their styles were so similar.

So much has been written in the past and recently on Mrs. Storm, that I will simply close my remarks about her by saying that she was a very strong willed woman and eventually she and Hamilton had a dispute and they parted company.

Now an established Sexton Blake writer, the war in 1914 saw him in Paris. Returning to London, he joined the King Edward's Horse, a Canadian troop, and served in France. Later he was stationed in Dublin, where he became very ill with pneumonia. Invalided out of the services, he was offered a post in French Cochin which he accepted and so did not resume his writing career. Possibly he thought that the hot climate on the west coast of Southern India would be far more beneficial to his health than the damp in England. It was here, as branch manager of an export firm, that he first met Mrs. Ivy Teed at a fancy dress ball, who incidentally was the daughter of a government official. They were married in 1920, and with the closing down of the export branches, Hamilton decided to resume his career in London writing Sexton Blake yarns, and so they arrived back in England in 1921.

After a short while, they moved over to France, where they lived in the Latin quarter in Paris. Mrs. Teed took a deep interest in her husband's writings and they often used to discuss plots. Hamilton's favourite character was that arch criminal Huxton Rymer, whilst he based Yvonne on his favourite actress star Yvonne Arnaud. He used to type his stories straight out with no pages ever wasted and no subbing afterwards. But above all he really enjoyed writing his Blake yarns, which is certainly different from some authors I have met who considered writing a grind, and more like an imposition. If any author ever influenced him it was obviously Michael Storm, and he used to enjoy talking about him and his writings. Not of course knowing that such interest would be shown about Michael Storm some 50 years later, Mrs. Teed unfortunately did not remember as much as she wished she had done at the time about this author — except to say that most certainly her husband had never met him, as he had died long before Hamilton ever contemplated writing Blakes.

Mrs. Teed can well remember Mr. H. W. Twyman coming to Paris to discuss a plot with Hamilton for a story. They went to a cathedral and became so engrossed in a theme for a plot that Hamilton picked up a jewelled scarab and put it in his pocket. It took a lot of explaining to the guide before things were back to normal!

Hamilton could speak French fluently, as he had learned it in his boyhood in Canada, where French is the second language. Surprisingly, he very rarely talked about his old home life and he eventually sold his shares in his father's business, after a sister had visited him in London. Hamilton, however, often brought his own real life adventures into his stories, and what man better than he with his vast experience in world travels, and with his various localities so authentic in colour.

Towards the end of the 1930s, however, Hamilton became very ill, and eventually died in London at Whitechapel, just before the war. Mrs. Teed has an old, now very tattered copy of the UNION JACK which her husband wrote, which has been read over and over again; and two bound books "Volcano Island" and "The Voodoo Queen", one of which is autographed and has a photograph of Hamilton in his prime inside the cover.

Memories not only of a husband but of probably the greatest Sexton Blake writer of them all.

© W. O. G. Lofts

1. TWO CROOKS FOR HOLLYWOOD.

MADAME VALI MATA-VALI sat in a long wicker chair beneath the sun awning on the after-deck of the small but beautifully lined steam yacht Thetis, smoking a thin Russian cigarette and gazing in lazy approval at her partner, George Marsden Plummer, who reclined in another chaise lounge opposite her.

Vali Mata-Vali was about as seductive a picture of feminine charm as one could conceive. Her frock of thin, clinging white seemed to be simple enough in its lines, but woman would have known after one glance that it was a rare and almost priceless confection from the inimitable Patou. Her slim and very shapely limbs were clad in white stockings of the finest silken gauze, while a high-arched small foot was shod in thin white buckskin.

With the tout ensemble of white as a direct contrast to her black hair and sloe-black, slightly oblique eyes she had achieved just that master touch that makes all the difference, and—she knew it. The only touch of colour in the whole scheme was in the faint flush of her cheeks and the ripe crimson of her lips.

She was beautiful and desirable, and as he gazed upon her, George Marsden Plummer congratulated himself afresh that Fate had dealt him such a perfect asset as a partner, for the beautiful actress who had set Paris aflame not long before—she had been known as the Bird of Paradise—had both brains and money as well as beauty, and, what was even more important to the master criminal, was prepared to "go the limit," so to say, if the prize to be gained warranted.

They were, as a matter of fact, about the most dangerous couple that could have come together with the sole intention of filching from Society in general, and any ripe prospect in particular, adequate reward for their adventurous activities.

Some months before, Plummer had been chafing in the fanatical city of Meknes away in the South of Morocco, casting about for something which would yield him sufficient loot to break once more into the arena of crime in Europe. Abdel-Krim, the Lion of the Riff, had fallen, and his captain of the front-line troops, Sakre-el-Drooge, the Hawk of the Peak—who was George Marsden Plummer—had found his services at a discount.

A pretty scheme which he had cooked up with one Beni Said, doyen of all rascals in Tangier—which means Morocco—had ended in a fizzle, due to the unwelcome interference of Sexton Blake.

Following that the coast ports had become too hot to hold Plummer, and, with Europe barred to him while he was next door to a pauper, he had journeyed south to Meknes, which at the time was the rendezvous of every devout Mahommedan in North Africa. There, in that wild press, he figured he might turn some chance to his advantage.

And to him in Meknes had come the beautiful Vali Mata-Vali to seek his aid. Even now, after he had been with her constantly for months, it seemed all but a wonderful dream to Plummer. She had come with money and jewels and—herself. Together they had embarked upon one of the most daring plots that criminal had ever conceived—nothing less than to secure five priceless pearls which had disappeared from the Temple of Eternal Purity which stands by the Gate of the Tiger in Canton and which were known as the Five Sacred Thimbles of Chentse.

How they actually got those fabulous jewels into their possession, and how they were snatched away by Sexton Blake in the very moment of victory, has been related in the famous "Index" at Baker Street under the Case Reference title of "The Tiger of Canton."

Following the conclusion of that affair at Vali Mata-Vali's chateau at St. Cloud on the outskirts of Paris the pair had found it expedient to fade away from the glare of publicity they had roused. Moreover, the chagrined inspectors from the Surete, Collet and Journet, who had actually had the handcuffed Plummer in their hands, were only too keen to establish contact with the master criminal once more.

London was, of course, too hot to hold them, and so, with that amazing resource which had already won Plummer's unstinted admiration, Vali Mata-Vali had whisked him away to the Eastern Mediterranean, and almost before he knew whither she was leading him, had established him aboard the luxurious yacht Thetis.

To say that Plummer had fallen on his feet was to put it mildly. Not for more than eight years, ever since he had first sought safety in the Riff country, had he known the ease of life which his association with the beautiful Vali Mata-Vali had given him.

The only care he had in the world was the necessity to avoid the police, and that hadn't proved very difficult with the speedy Thetis to carry them from the zone of danger.

Nor was Vali Mata-Vali dissatisfied with the arrangement, despite the failure of the affair in Paris. Until she had found Plummer in Meknes she had known him only by name; but on that moonlight night when Plummer had come to her by way of a silken ladder and stood before her in white tunic edged with crimson, his forked black beard and jewel-hilted sword stamping him as a true savage warrior, whatever else he might have been— his dominating masculinity so completely in contrast to the dancing puppets she had known in Paris and his readiness to tackle anything she suggested had won her completely in that night of romance.

Since then she had given him a love as savage and passionate as his own wild nature could have desired, and during those months just passed the two had led a lotus-eating existence the while they cruised at will about the warm waters of the Mediterranean.

And on this morning as she lay regarding Plummer lazily, Vali Mata-Vali was thinking that she had been lucky to bring this man under her dominion. He certainly was a good looking animal as he lay there, sprawled out in the long chair, clad in heavy Shantung silk, his face and hands almost mahogany coloured through those years of rough campaigning in the Riff, his eyes cold and steely despite the lowered lids.

Now was gone the forked beard that had stamped Sakre-el-Drooge among the tribes of the Riff and the Jabala; instead it had been trimmed to a neat point in deference to the more orthodox ideas of civilisation.

At the moment the Thetis was riding at anchor in Tripoli harbour. They had come across from a long cruise among the isles of the Aegean, and now with the gateway of the dangerous west close at hand Vali Mata-Vali was occupying her mind with plans for the immediate future.

Until that morning she had been content to postpone any thought of action; she had been happy in just letting the lazy, sunny days pass unheeded. But among the big batch of letters which she had collected in Tripoli was one which had given her to think, and it was the line of thought leading her to speak of future plans to Plummer.

She smiled faintly as she saw him pour out a fresh glass of chilled wine and nibble a thin biscuit. Plummer always had revelled in the "flesh-pots," and there had been no need to stint himself since he had been with Vali Mata-Vali. She had given without reservation, and

3

it gave her a pleasant thrill to watch the evident enjoyment of this big, healthy animal in the good things which her wealth had provided.

She waited until he set the empty glass down with a sigh of content and had lighted a cigarette; then she spoke:

"How long since you have been in America, mon ami?"

Plummer cast an interested eye at her, pausing to let his gaze sweep slowly over her form before replying. Then:

"About ten years, Vali; why?"

"Have you ever been in Hollywood?"

"The place in California which has been developed by the motion-picture people—yes. I had rather a hectic week there to tell the truth. But that was a few years back. Have you been there?"

"No. but I was considering if we should go there. I have had a letter this morning which I shall tell you of!"

Plummer sat up. He knew from the tone of her voice that the nebulous fabric of an idea was in her mind, and, so far as he was concerned, he was quite ready to tackle some new scheme, particularly if the scene of action promised to be as far distant from the police of London and Paris as this place Hollywood of which she had spoken.

She had extracted a letter from a white doeskin bag that was hanging from the arm of her chair, and now, spreading out several sheets of paper on her knee, she began to read it to him.

It was a communication from one of the biggest motion-picture directors in Hollywood, and had been sent to her at the Grande Theatre in Paris. Her faithful agent in Paris—who had been driven nearly frantic by her abrupt repudiation of all her contracts, but who kept hoping that she would recover from this fit of madness and return—had forwarded it on. It contained an offer to the actress to appear in three major films at Hollywood exclusively under the direction of the director in question, the three scenarios to be submitted to Vali for her approval, all three to be made during the course of twelve months, or over a longer period if she elected, and her remuneration to be the sum of one million francs down, all possible expenses she should incur—including her house and servants while in Hollywood—and a fifty per cent royalty on the American and foreign receipts of each picture.

It was, as a business proposition, one that the most haughty actress would find it necessary to pause and consider. It meant a fortune of considerable size even in these days of colossal salaries paid to film stars, and, did she choose to tackle it on a strictly business basis, Vali Mata-Vali could have added enormously to her already comfortable resources.

But that letter did not affect her as the impresario who had written it had intended. It had the effect of throwing her thoughts in the direction of Hollywood, and the association of ideas recalled to her mind a certain American multi-millionaire who had visited Paris while she was creating a furore at the Grande.

This gentleman, with the outspoken frankness which characterises his race, had made no bones about telling the actress that he had "fallen for her good and hard"; that he could rub "quite a few millions together," and that he "would be tickled to death" if she would relieve him of one of his cheque-books and become Mrs. Peter J. Constant."

He was constant by name and constant by nature, and he'd show her proof of that, despite the fact that he had already been married and divorced three times.

It was not any fear of embarking on such a well-travelled matrimonial sea that had deterred Vali from accepting his offer. At the time there had been a dozen others, equally as rich and certainly more polished, at her feet. Money meant nothing to her, for she already had plenty, and could get more from each of those sources by the mere crooking of one of her shapely little fingers.

Therefore Mr. Peter J. Constant had failed in his laudable efforts to make her the fourth Mrs. Constant, but even then he had taken the pains to send her his address in case she ever changed her mind. And that address had shown that Mr. Peter J. Constant lived in Hollywood.

When she had read the letter to Plummer, she told him the history of her acquaintance with the multimillionaire, and when she had finished glanced at him roguishly.

"What do you say, mon ami? Shall we commission the Thetis for the voyage across the Atlantic? We could get sufficient here in Tripoli, and go through the Panama Canal. It would be amusing to arrive in this barbarous Hollywood in such fashion, and, who knows? we might make the visit more profitable. I took the trouble to ascertain that this crazy American who calls himself in such impossible fashion, really is a person of great wealth. I was informed that he owned almost half of Hollywood, so that we should give him great wealth."

Plummer nodded slowly.

"It sounds all right, Vali. Seems to me I have heard of Peter J. Constant. But what about the offer from Schwarz, the impresario?"

She snapped her fingers.

"Pouf! I care not that for his offer! When we get there we can decide. You shall say 'Yes' or 'No.' It might be fun to appear in one picture. I have never done so. I have always thought I should like to appear in 'La Dame aux Camellias,' but, then, that was clone so perfectly on the legitimate stage by Bernhardt, and on the screen by Nazimova—though I could do it better than she."

"I am perfectly certain you could," responded Plummer quickly. He was a wise man in his generation, was George Marsden Plummer, and he knew what reply had been expected of him. There was no susceptibilities in all the human race to equal those of a successful actress or prima donna.

She smiled her approval of his words, and went on:

"As for you, dear friend, you shall be the manager of Madame Vali Mata-Vali; is it not so?"

"I was wondering where I came in on this," murmured Plummer.

"There will be plenty for you to do. It is you who must think of some scheme by which we can separate the fat Mr. Peter J. Constant from some of his millions. Nothing less will do."

"Millions!"

The master criminal uttered the word lovingly. It rolled off his tongue much as a bit of whipped cream would have been rolled about the palate of a schoolgirl.

"Millions! I think, Vali, if I make a study of all you can tell me about this bird, Constant, I shall be able to figure out some way of prying a few millions loose before we finish with him."

"Then you agree?"

Plummer nodded, and reached for a fresh pint of champagne.

"We cross the Atlantic as soon as you are ready."

And thus was originated one of the biggest jolts that Hollywood the notorious was to experience for many a long day.

2.   The Millionaire of Hollywood.

MR. PETER J. CONSTANT, of Los Angeles and Hollywood, had not overstated his case when he boasted to Vali Mata-Vali in Paris that he was a multi-millionaire. Even if he were so counted in dollars, the sum total of his realisable investments would have been sufficient to place him among the European multi-millionaires in sterling, which is sufficient proof that he was a very rich man.

And he had made every dollar by his own acuteness of mind.

Thirty years ago, when the city of Los Angeles was just beginning to experience the spectacular boom which sent the prices of its real estate soaring to heights previously undreamed of on the Pacific coast of America, Mr. Peter J. Constant—just plain Pete in those days—had drifted in from the Nevada silver mines with three or four thousand dollars in his jeans.

To acquire even a small parcel of Los Angeles real estate was the very last thought in his mind. But a couple of blocks on the outskirts of the city had come into his possession via that interesting game of cards known as draw poker, and, somewhat to his amazement, he had a chance, three days later, of cashing them in for nearly five times as much as he had accepted them for across the poker table.

Until then, Pete Constant had been just a rough-and-tumble prospector, sometimes possessing a few hundreds, but more often than not finding it a considerable exercise of his ingenuity to wheedle someone into grub-staking him for a trip into the mountains. For the very first time in his life he experienced the thrill that comes with the realisation that one is a landholder—a solid citizen, so to speak.

It was this flush of newly acquired dignity that caused Pete Constant to refuse the offer for his lots—that had cost him no more than the effort to draw two cards that had given him a useful "full house" —and to begin to make inquiries into just what this fever was that seemed to have seized the whole city of Los Angeles.

Of all "bugs" known to civilisation there is none that gets a man harder than the bite of the real estate boom, as witness the recent wild boom in Florida, and the subsequent slump which has ruined thousands. By the time Pete Constant had found the blocks that he possessed, and had listened to a few of the tales of prophecy regarding what Los Angeles was going to be ten years hence, he was infected with the deadly bacillus. Instead of selling, he bought more blocks, and still more, and again more.

When almost every dollar he possessed was sunk in bare lots of land, he sat back and waited. Nor was he disappointed. The offers began to roll in, and he sold methodically. By the time he had disposed of his first collection he had trebled his original stake. In three months he had cleaned up a cool hundred thousand dollars; and then he stuck his stake in for keeps.

He never looked back. When Hollywood was nothing but a name and a few coloured squares on the posters of the land-selling companies, Pete Constant bought right and left—secured title to stretches of barren land that brought chuckles of glee into the throats of those who took him for a "sucker."

But Constant went on his way quietly, and when Hollywood sprang into fame as the most ideal place in all America for the making of motion pictures, owing to the wonderful clearness of the atmosphere and the special qualities of the sunlight, the value of his holdings went up by leaps and bounds.

The big companies simply had to have his blocks, which they found included the most perfect situations in all Hollywood. Well, they got them at a price, but not the freehold.

Constant, who was now Peter J gave out short-term leases at what was considered hold-up prices. He kept the freehold to himself, and three years later, when those leases ran out, he renewed them at exactly five times the original figure he had demanded. And again they were for three years only, with option of renewal at his figure. He had them coming and going, and he played them to a standstill.

Hollywood simply had to grow, and while he owned that land, Peter J. Constant could no more help becoming a millionaire many times over than a movie actress can help telling herself each morning what a beautiful creature she is, and how infinitely superior to every other actress in Hollywood the world must consider her.

It took twenty years to put Peter J. Constant in that position, and after that he did little but watch his holdings rise and rise, and keep on rising in value while he sat back and clipped coupons from the great piles of gilt-edged bonds that was growing higher every year.

By the time he made the "grand tour" of Europe, Peter J. Constant could be reckoned one of the thirty richest men in America, and that is saying something. He was a director in half the big banks and businesses on the Pacific coast; his financial strings reached as far east as New York. He had arrived.

During this voyage on the swelling seas of wealth, Constant had adventured three different times along the tricky matrimonial rapids. Each attempt had ended in the divorce court with a substantial sum as alimony to salve the wounded feelings of the discarded lady. Yet, to be fair to Constant, he was no more to blame than the women. They had one and all been gold-diggers at best.

The wonderful beauty and extraordinary charm of Vali Mata-Vali had made a deep impression on him. She was unlike any woman he had ever known. There was a smooth line to her slender figure that reminded him of a thoroughbred horse; there was a finish to her manners that had been entirely lacking in the preceding three Mrs. Constants.

She was, to him, literally a bird of paradise, and he figured that he could buy her with a few millions of his money. He had never yet failed to get anything he wanted if he bid high enough.

But he hadn't been able to buy even a smile from Vali Mata-Vali. Had that extremely clever little lady not been surfeited with the attentions of a dozen other rich men, she might have amused herself by watching the antics of this middle-aged, boastful man from the Far West.

To Vali he was like some strange animal. She had never come into contact with that type of man any more than he had ever crossed the path of a finished woman like herself—the last word, as it were, in what effete Europe and specialised civilisation could produce.

She had been perfectly aware, however, that she had made a deep and genuine impression on him. And it was but natural that he should come into her mind when she read the letter from Schwarz, the impresario. But now Peter J. Constant existed in her thoughts solely as a something which might be used to the joint advantage of herself and Plummer.

For the first time in her life, Vali Mata-Vali had surrendered completely to a man, and, in doing so, had given with a fierceness that made up for the years of trifling which had preceded this affair. It was the "grande passion" with her, and she would fight with and for Plummer like a tigress.

What she did not know, though, was that since his return to Hollywood, Peter J. Constant had married for the fourth time. Despite his infatuation for the beautiful actress he had seen in Paris, he had not dedicated the rest of his life to single blessedness and the worship of her image in the inner shrine of his heart.

Peter J. Constant was the sort that simply could not live without the close companionship of a woman, and in less than three months after he had laid his much-battered heart and many millions at the feet of Vali Mata-Vali, he was joined in the bonds of Californian wedlock to a very shrewd and farsighted lady of Polish birth, who was, at the time, one of the most brilliant stars in the Hollywood movie constellation.

Peter J. Constant had bitten off one of the biggest mouthfuls of his whole life when he married Sonia Vensky, but he didn't know it yet.

She was certainly beautiful, and graced his table fittingly, even if she had been but a café dancer in Warsaw before a prowling American movie scout saw her. That suited Constant down to the ground. He liked to see something ornamental opposite him, and he could afford to pay for the pleasure.

Moreover, he was a free spender. He had never dropped his early habit of sitting in at a game of poker, but now, instead of playing for hundreds, he would only hold a hand with "the roof off."

He had a magnificent ten-room apartment on the sixteenth floor of the Imperial Hotel in Los Angeles, a marvellous Spanish mission bungalow in fifty acres of amazing gardens in Hollywood, a very secluded little place some twelve miles out of Hollywood on the coast, where he gave private stag parties and down in the Gulf of California, a whole island of his own where he had converted an old Spanish monastery into the most wonderful fishing lodge on the Pacific coast.

Horses for polo which he never used; hacks which he rode to death; a fleet of motor-cars at each of his places, and an oil-burning yacht that could show her heels to a trans-Atlantic greyhound. He was well fixed, and on the face of it, was an excellent prospect for plucking by Vali Mata-Vali had it not been for the newest Mrs. Constant. Just why this should be will appear as the present conditions of Peter J. Constant's life are revealed.

Now that corpulent gentleman had no suspicion, when he walked out on to the veranda of his secluded little place on the coast south of Hollywood one morning after a particularly hectic stag party, that the small, but beautifully built white yacht that was anchored about three hundred yards off shore and nearly opposite his bungalow could have on board anyone who would possess a personal interest for him. He was still sleepy as he rubbed his eyes and reached mechanically for a pair of binoculars.

"Thetis."

He could read the name quite clearly, but on the stern he could only make out under Thetis the latter part of the name of the port of registration. This gave him the letters N-D-R-I-A. He was a keen yachtsman, and well acquainted with every port of registration in America. But he could not think of one at the moment which ended in those letters. Nor did he recognise the burgee which flew at the mast-head—a red and white burgee it was, with the initials "A.Y.C." on it.

The Y.C. was plain enough. That could only mean yacht club; but what port began with A and ended in N-D-R-1-A? He couldn't place it, so, losing interest for the moment, he toddled along, clad only in his pyjamas, to the hedged-in private swimming-pool for his morning dip.

But later, as he sat on the wide piazza, devouring his fresh iced cantaloupe and waffles, with golden maple syrup, hot rolls and fragrant coffee, Peter J. Constant made a closer study of the beautiful Thetis. Now and then he would lay down his implements and reach for the glasses. He could catch fleeting glimpses of two white-clad figures pacing the after-deck—a tall, bearded man and a woman.

There was something familiar about the woman, it seemed, but it was not until he had finished breakfast and took up his position in the private look-out known as the "crow's-nest" that he made out her features plainly. And then it was that Peter J. Constant gave vent to a low whistle of amazement.

"Vali Mata-Vali, by all that's priceless," he ejaculated. "Now what has brought her to the Pacific coast and who the deuce is the man with her? This has got to be looked into at once."

From which it will be seen that Peter J. Constant had not even paused to consider what the fourth Mrs. Constant, safe for the moment in the great house in Hollywood, might have to say on the same subject.

3. Dangerous Complications.

PETER J. CONSTANT acted with his usual promptitude.

Inside ten minutes he was seated in the stern-sheets of his speedy forty-foot motor-boat on his way to the Thetis. His crew of four all wore the Constant yachting uniform, and even as the boat swept in towards the yacht the accommodation-ladder was being lowered, for his approach had been witnessed.

Half-way from the shore the millionaire had been able to make out all the lettering in the name of the port of registration— Alexandria. That must be Egypt, he thought, and he puzzled to know why, if the craft belonged to Vali Mata-Vali, the reason she should have it registered out of an Egyptian port. Then it occurred to him that the tall, bearded man with her might conceivably be her husband.

In that case he might be an unwelcome guest if they were on their honeymoon; and, certainly, she had not been married when he had seen her in Paris, despite the fact that she had been given the courtesy title of "madame."

But his qualms soon passed in the intensity of his desire to gaze once more into those deep, sloe-black eyes that had enthralled him in the City of Light. Everything he had felt then came back upon him now with a rush, and by the time he reached the deck he was eager to touch her hand as any youth suffering the tortures of calflove. The fourth Mrs. Constant had completely vanished from his thoughts.

Needless to say, Vali Mata-Vali and Plummer had watched his approach. Now it was sheer coincidence that the "Thetis" should have lain off the millionaire's bungalow during the preceding night. When it was plain that they could not reach a point off Los Angeles before dusk, Plummer and Vali had decided to anchor, and steam into port the following day.

They had planned the opening of the campaign which had begun with a letter to Schwarz—posted at Tripoli— advising him that Madame Vali Mata-Vali would arrive within a few weeks in Hollywood in order, personally, to discuss his offer, and then, silence, until a wireless had been sent just after they passed through the Panama Canal, informing him that she was on her way in her private yacht and would arrive at Los Angeles on such-and-such a day.

On this morning when Peter J. Constant had seen the yacht it had been Vali's intention to send a further message to Schwarz, inviting him to lunch on board, and then, when liaison had been established with that well-known producer, so to say—proof of the actress' motive in coming to Hollywood—they could begin to take up the matter of Peter J. Constant.

But this unexpected arrival of the millionaire made a change in their plans necessary, and while he sped towards them Plummer and Vali were cooking up just what they would say.

Despite his renewed infatuation, the millionaire was observant enough to take note of the captain and crew of the yacht. They were, he saw at once, either Levantines or Greeks, with the exception of about a dozen or so whose hooked noses and swarthy skins proclaimed Arab blood.

If he had known that the tall, bearded man beside Vali was none other but the notorious Sakre-el-Drooge who had fought as captain of the front-line troops under Abdel-Krim in the Riff country, and that these Arab-looking fellows were direct descendants of the corsairs of old who had made the Barbary Coast a terror to every nation in Europe, he might have paused long enough to wonder why a pleasure craft should carry such a crew.

But to Peter J. Constant they were just a pack of "niggers," and so he passed them, eyes aflame with eagerness to greet Vali Mata-Vali.

She received him graciously, expressing a suitable measure of surprise at his coming. Then she introduced Plummer as Senor Jorge Machado, her distant relative and director of affairs, at which announcement Peter J. Constant lost the throbbings of jealousy which had been in his breast ever since he had seen Plummer. Her relative and manager—well, that was all right.

As they moved aft to where wicker chairs and tables had been placed the millionaire explained how it was he had ventured out.

"I could scarcely believe my eyes, madame," he said, as he sank back and accepted one of Plummer's cigars. "I said to myself: 'It is'; then I said, 'No, impossible.' But I was right, and I could not wait longer to pay my respects. It is indeed a great pleasure to see you in California, and I trust you are planning to remain some time."

Vali smiled her most bewitching smile.

She was determined that he should become imbued with a fervent desire that she should remain for a long time. She did not know about the fourth Mrs. Constant.

"I expect to be here for some weeks, perhaps months—perhaps longer," she said sweetly. "I was going to send you a note as soon as we reached Los Angeles. You see, cher ami, I have not forgotten that when you were in Paris you told me it would give you pleasure to show me your wonderful California. And, so, you will have the opportunity. Is it not so?"

Peter J. Constant suddenly recollected that he had a wife to consider.

He gulped in sudden embarrassment. He had not been married very long, but he had learned enough in that time to know that the fourth Mrs. Constant professed a terrible jealousy where he was concerned, and had the temper of a fiend.

Just how she would regard his acquisition of such a young and beautiful protege as this—of an actress who was famous in Europe in a way that no fame in Hollywood could equal, was a problem to which he couldn't guess the answer.

And his embarrassment might have been considerably deeper if he had known that, at that very moment, his wife was starting from Hollywood to motor to the bungalow in company with her pet cavalier, the soulful Paolo Posani, her leading man in soulful love episodes, and, privately, a dangerous devil who had had murder in his heart ever since she had laughed and married Peter J. Constant for his millions.

He had sworn to possess her, and it was this human factor in the form of Paolo Posani which was to become a major static interference, so to speak, in the plans of Vali Mata-Vali and George Marsden Plummer.

Indeed, there was brewing beneath the warm sunshine of that Californian coast a first-class drama which was to end in a blaze of notoriety which was to shock even blasé Hollywood.

"Er—I do hope you will remain a long time," stammered Peter J. Constant. "Er—um, I should be most happy if you and your—er—cousin, Senor Machado, will come ashore and lunch with me to-day."

Vali glanced towards Plummer, whose right eye flickered almost imperceptibly; then she nodded.

"We should be delighted, Mr. Constant."

"Shall we say half-past twelve? I will send the motor-boat for you."

"We shall be ready."

Then the millionaire switched the conversation off to the subject of fishing. He was feeling quite friendly now to Plummer, particularly so, because he did not want to have the talk hang about his private affairs and what he had been doing since he had left Vali in Paris. He wanted time to think how he should break the news to her, for broken it must be.

Nevertheless, he was determined that the possession of a wife should not stand in the way of his devoting himself to this woman who had affected him as no other woman. Hang Sonia and her devilish temper anyway, he was thinking. But perhaps she would find her match in this cool, self-possessed woman of the world.

Well, anyway, he wasn't going to let the Bird of Paradise slip through his fingers this time; he would manage it all some way. Which goes to show that Peter J. Constant was perfectly unscrupulous when his desires were in the ascendant. And as this is the tale of the deep play of passions among conscienceless people the truth must be portrayed.

By the time he had finished bragging to Plummer about the gigantic barracuda which could be caught in the Gulf of California, of fish running to three and four hundred-weight and caught on the hook and line, it was time for him to return and give orders regarding lunch. So, still making no mention of the fourth Mrs. Constant, he took his departure, promising to send the motor-boat a little after twelve.

"Something upset him," mused Vali, as they watched the little boat dancing away shorewards. "I wonder what it was?"

Plummer smiled.

"Do you mean when he swallowed lumps in his throat?"

"Yes; you noticed it?"

"I did. Your statement that you intended remaining for some time on the coast, and your reminder of what he had said to you in Paris, seemed to cause the phenomenon. Methinks our friend is keeping something back, but there is no doubt, Vali, my dear, that he is as head over heels in love with you as a sick sheep."

She shot him a look, and laid her fingers on his arm.

"You needn't worry. No one in the world counts but you."

And Plummer knew that she spoke the truth.

As for Peter J. Constant, he reached his bungalow in a state of ferment. Yelling for Soto, his Japanese servant, he gave that yellow-faced paragon orders for a lunch that would have pleased Lucullus.

15

Then he began pacing up and down the side veranda which was screened from the yacht, trying to figure out how he should break the news of his marriage to Vali Mata-Vali.

He was no coward, and he had no false ideas of women; but, all the same, he had deliberately funked springing the news on her when on board, and now he resolved to do the job by medium of a letter which she could read before coming ashore.

Seating himself at the big mission desk in the living-room, he made half a dozen attempts before he was satisfied. And. twenty minutes later, the following is what the amazed Vali read in her cabin:

"Dear Lady,—How can I convey to you what seeing you again to-day has meant to me? I have been the most arrant fool in the world. I believed what you said in Paris, and forced myself to run away from you. I could not bear being near you and yet so far away from you. I have tried in every way to forget, even to the extent of marrying again. And now the sight of you has roused all I felt before with added torture. I am in an agony of fear that you may think this alters things; but it needn't. I am, as I have always been,
"Your devoted slave,
"P. J. C."

It was extravagantly worded, but Peter J. Constant knew he had to go the whole hog if he wrote anything. The first hint Plummer had that such a missive had been received was when he heard the distant peal of Vali's silvery laughter, and then he saw her coming along the deck, holding the letter in her hand. She was choking with mirth.

"Read it!" she gasped. "There is constant love for you. He is married."

And Plummer read. But he did not laugh. On the contrary, he scratched his cheek thoughtfully.

"This rather complicates matters," he remarked, after a little while. "It is one thing to pry a gink loose from his money when he is unattached and infatuated, but it is quite another matter when he has a wife who may have deep fingers into his pile. I wonder what the wife is like?"

"Tant pis, mon ami! Why need we care? This but makes it the more interesting. And what, do you not think I am the equal of any other woman?"

Plummer sent her a level glance.

"There can be no possible question on that score, Vali; but, unless I am mistaken, this means we must figure out an entirely new plan of campaign. I am a pretty old stager at the gentle game of separating a man from his money, and my experience has been that the presence of a woman always complicates things."

"Then what of me?"

"I assure you that until you came to me in Meknes I had never even contemplated working with one of your sex. I have always been too afraid. That is why I have played a lone hand, and is probably why I managed to elude the police as long as I did. But you are different. Do you imagine that this wife, no matter if she is young and pretty, or old and ugly as sin, is going to stand idly by while you fascinate and trim her husband?"

"No, of course not. But if the complications become very serious we can deal with them."

As she finished speaking her eyes rested on his. They gazed thus in silence at each other for a full half-minute, the woman asking a question and the man answering it. Their conversation was as perfectly understood between them as if it had been spoken audibly. And in that moment George Marsden Plummer knew that if things came to the point where killing must be done, they would not stop at that.

He shrugged as he rose.

"It shall be as you wish, my dear. You will find me ready for any eventuality."

"And I am ready to go any limit— with you!" she breathed.

A deadly and terribly dangerous pair to be free to roam at large.

But their faces showed nothing of their thoughts as they sat in the stern-sheets of the motor-boat which had been sent to bring them ashore. Vali looked as demure and fetching as one could conceive; Plummer was grave and dignified, a model manager for the illustrious actress.

They found their host waiting at the jetty to welcome them. His eyes were hot and eager as he sought Vali's. What he saw there was a smile that sent his doubts flying, and he was almost idiotic in his clumsy relief as he assisted her out of the boat. It was with a well-feigned air of carelessness that he announced that there would be others for lunch, as his wife had just motored out from Hollywood with a friend.

"I shall be interested to meet the wife of my old friend," said Vali lightly. "Is it perhaps that she has been connected with the moving-picture screen?"

"Oh, yes! She is rather well known; is making a picture now, in fact. Perhaps you have heard of Sonia Vensky?"

Vali Mata-Vali raised her brows in genuine surprise. She had heard of the famous and, reputedly, very temperamental film star, Sonia Vensky; and, in fact, had seen her on one occasion at a private view in Paris. So this was the wife with whom she had to tilt!

"But yes," she responded vivaciously, "who has not heard of the famous and beautiful Sonia Vensky? You are indeed a lucky man, monsieur, to have won the hand of so fair a lady!"

Peter J. Constant's grunt might have meant anything, but he was spared the necessity of a reply, for by now they were close to the steps leading up to the piazza, and a few moments later he was presenting Vali Mata-Vali to Sonia Vensky, a red-headed beauty with eyes that were like the points of twin daggers.

Then Paolo Posani stepped forward, and at the sight of the dark, effeminate-looking fellow with artifically waved hair, George Marsden Plummer knew in a flash the secret of the triangle of human passions against which he and Vali had stumbled.

Outwardly he was suave and mildly amiable; inwardly his mind was working fast, trying to get the exact balance of each human factor before him, so that he might anticipate what one or all might do under certain desperate circumstances.

But it was a little later that the master criminal needed every atom of self-control to refrain from betraying the sudden amaze that filled him when Soto, the Japanese houseboy, came out to announce that lunch was served. For the barest fraction of a second his eyes met Plummer's full, but not by the flicker of an eyelash did he give any sign that he may have seen this bearded man before.

And yet, as sure as he sat there, Plummer was positive that the last time he had seen this same Jap was stripped to the waist in Dutch Pete's gin dive in Banjermasin, that mephitic hole away down in the south-west corner of Borneo. The following morning the Jap had disappeared from the settlement,— and a little later they had found, in an upstairs room of the dive, the body of a European, who had come in on a schooner a week before with a score of marketable pearls in his waist-belt. The fellow's throat had been slit from ear to ear, and what remained of the pearls had disappeared with the Jap.

4. The First Move.

PLUMMER had no time at lunch to ponder on the mystery of Soto, even though he kept surreptitious watch on the boy while he served. He found that he needed all his wits to follow the opening fire in the duel that was already beginning between Vali Mata-Vali and Sonia Vensky. It would almost seem as if Sonia Vensky had scented some secret understanding between her husband and the French actress, for the subtle acidity of her remarks were too vicious to be due entirely to professional jealousy.

Plummer left the battle in Vali's hands. He hadn't the slightest doubt that she could be more than a match for the Polish woman. After all, when temper should strip the veneer from Sonia Vensky, there remained nothing but the coarse and profane girl of the low-class cafe, while, despite her criminal proclivities, Vali Mata-Vali was the quintessence of breeding and European culture in every fibre of her being. Did the duel remain verbal, she would soon reduce the Polish woman to pulp—metaphorically speaking.

Besides, Plummer was anxious to make a more careful study of the millionaire and the Italian film star. He had little difficulty in classifying Constant; he had dealt with scores of men similar in their simple desires and the wherewithal to gratify them.

But Posani puzzled him. Those eyes told a tale to Plummer, who had made it his business to learn how to read a man by what looked out of his head. There was in them a fire that told the master criminal here was a man who would stop at nothing if his passions were roused.

At the moment he was suave enough, and, it was plain, was full of conceit, for whenever he had a chance he talked with sickening self-assurance of his "art," and of what a masterpiece the world would see in the new film which he and Sonia Vensky were making.

It was here that Plummer thought he would drop a small bomb, for up to now not even Constant knew that Vali Mata-Vali had been offered a contract by the great impresario, Morris Schwarz, the terms of which would set all Hollywood agog when they were made public.

"This is all very interesting and new to me," he remarked, in precise, scarcely accented English. "May I, dear cousin"—and here he glanced towards Vali, who nodded—"may I reveal to these very good friends of ours your little secret?"

He had them all interested at once, and then he imparted the information that they had come from the Mediterranean in the Thetis in order to have a personal interview with Morris Schwarz, who had made his cousin an offer of such magnitude that not even she, the Bird of Paradise, could find it in her heart to ignore it. Both Sonia Vensky and Paolo Posani fixed jealous eyes on Vali.

It had been no little shock to Sonia Vensky to discover that this fascinating creature who had dropped out of the sky so opportunely for her husband to entertain her, was none other than the world-famous Bird of Paradise.

Even while she had been sending out her little shafts the Polish woman had been thinking hard. Was it only chance, she kept asking herself, that the yacht had come to anchor directly opposite her husband's bungalow? Or had he known of her coming?

She remembered now that she had heard him mention something about meeting Vali Mata-Vali when he had been in Paris, and while she never appeared when he gave his stag parties at the bungalow she was beginning to wonder now if the party the night before had been all a bluff. Her violent jealousy and antipathy to Vali were in full swing while Paolo Posani drew out particulars of her offer from Schwarz.

It did not make them any easier in mind that the same Morris Schwarz was the impresario under whom they were both appearing in their new scenario, "Love Madness," and Plummer privily told himself it was safe betting that there would be an upheaval when the terms which Morris Schwarz had offered Vali became known.

Within six hours that secluded bungalow had become a centre of intrigue. In each mind there was spinning a scheme which could not help but touch one or all of the others in some way. Four souls there were at that table, speaking with the tongue of convention, but which, in reality, were seething with greed and lust and hate.

Ever Peter J. Constant was scheming how he could make love to Vali Mata-Vali and avoid an open rupture with his wife. There were present the first-class makings of heavy drama, and when those passions broke their bounds, something was certain to happen.

Somewhat to Plummer's surprise, Constant's wife announced almost immediately after lunch that she would motor back into Hollywood. She pleaded the necessity to appear at a short "set" at the studio later in the afternoon, and, of course, Posani would accompany her.

Almost immediately following this she ordered the car, and, after a polite lie that she should hope for the pleasure of seeing much more of Vali Mata-Vali and her cousin, Senor Machado, she and Posani disappeared.

Peter J. Constant heaved a genuine sigh of relief when they were gone, and would have kept his two guests until after tea, but Vali, playing some game of her own, expressed their regret and insisted on returning to the yacht. She promised to give him an appointment in Los Angeles, and before he could mumble any protests, she was tripping away with Plummer, a little puzzled at this new turn, following.

Constant saw them off at the jetty, and stood watching until they were on their way up the accommodation ladder.

The moment they were on deck Vali turned to Plummer.

"Come aft, mon ami. I have a suggestion to make."

When they were seated on opposite sides of a cane table she bent her eyes on him.

"What do you think of it?"

"More complicated than ever, Vali. The woman is no fool, and she hates you like poison. The man is crazy about her, and would knife Constant if she but gave the word. Even without us there is trouble brewing among those three."

"Bien. I had noticed the same thing. But it makes things better in one way for us. I think, mon ami, there should be material enough in that situation for us to plan something even more subtle than we had discussed. Did you notice the Japanese servant?"

Plummer glanced at her in surprise. "Yes—and I know him."

It was Vali's turn to lift her brows. "Know him—what do you mean?"

"I knew that yellow man in a certain place in the East Indies some years ago. He slit the throat of a European from ear to ear and got away with some pearls the poor chap had on him."

"Tiens! Are you certain?"

"I never make mistakes of that sort."

"That is important. Do you know what I saw when the woman was leaving?"

"What?"

"I saw her pass that Japanese servant something which he thrust inside his coat—deeper than that, under his shirt."

"Could you see what it was?"

"No; it was something she could conceal in the palm of her hand. But there is an understanding between her and the Jap. He is probably a spy on her husband."

"He may be more than that," muttered Plummer. "You said you had a suggestion, Vali."

"Yes, and it seems to me even more worth while now after what you have just told me. It is that we send word ashore to Peter Constant that we shall remain anchored here to-night owing to some slight trouble with the engines. We shall invite him to dinner on board, and after I shall take care of him in the saloon while you go ashore to the bungalow. It would not be easy to think up an excuse, but I arranged for that before we left. I allowed my gold cigarette case to slip under the cushion of the chair on which I was sitting; that will be your excuse. Then you can make use of the brief time you will have with the Jap. I have a feeling that we could discover much of value from him if he could be made to talk."

"You leave that to me," responded Plummer grimly. "I'll make that yellow skin talk, or I'll wring his neck."

5.   Plummer's Methods.

SOTO, the Japanese houseboy, was standing in his master's room arranging his bed for the night when he heard a soft step on the veranda. The Japanese paused in the act of turning down the sheet and stood listening.

He did not turn his head, nor did his body twist in the direction of the sound. But his oblique eyes came over slowly, ever so slowly until they were mere pin points in the corners of the slits. He was as motionless as a statue, not the faintest wisp of breath seemed to be passing in and out of his lungs. Then:

"Nodo!"

Low but clear the word reached him. Still he did not move. If it were possible the eye slits narrowed more than ever, and suddenly, the pulse in his throat began to hammer out against the skin.

"Nodo!"

From the veranda, through the big living-room and past the curtains that hung over the bed-room door came that remorseless voice. The Jap allowed the pillow to slide softly on to the bed, and his eyes came back to the opposite corner of the slits so that he could look towards the open window. And still his feet remained fastened to the floor.

"Nodo—you dog, come hither, or I'll flay you alive."

The pulse in the Jap's throat hammered more violently than ever. Now his body relaxed, and one hand went up his sleeve so that the fingers curled round the handle of a knife that was strapped there. He withdrew the weapon stealthily, and thrust it inside his coat into some place that held it. But still he did not shift his feet until:

"Nodo—this is the last command."

Then the Jap began shuffling towards the door. He pushed the curtains aside and continued on through the living-room to the wide open french window that was the nearest means of exit to the piazza.

There in the gloom stood a tall, powerfully built figure. It was the bearded man who had come ashore from the yacht that day. Over his shoulder Soto could see the yacht, outlined in fairy lights as she rose superbly at anchor, seemingly but a biscuit toss from the shore. Soto's master was there, and the bearded man was here!

"You have called someone, master," said the Jap in calm tones. "I, Soto, am only servant in bungalow to-night."

"You—Soto! You dog, Nodo, how did you get here?"

"Soto not know what the master talk of. Soto know no Jap boy called Nodo. Soto all alone in bungalow."

George Marsden Plummer took a swift step forward and shot out one hand. His powerful fingers closed over the Jap's wrist, and with the other he tore open the boy's white coat. His white teeth showed in a snarl as he saw the knife which had been thrust into a deep strap inside. He had it out with a deft twist and sent it spinning over the rail of the veranda.

Next he ripped Soto's shirt open in one single sweep of the hand, and a low oath escaped him as something fell at his feet. He bent swiftly to pick it up, holding the Jap firmly while he did so. His fingers encountered a folded bit of crisp paper, and then, when he spread it out, even Plummer's eyes widened in amazement.

What he held was a yellow-backed note for one thousand dollars. And this was what Sonia Vensky had passed surreptitiously to the Jap before leaving that afternoon!

Plummer thrust the note into his own pocket and dragged the Jap to the rail. Holding him so that the last bit of dying light in the west fell full upon his throat he peered at the place where that pulse throbbed. Again his teeth showed in a snarl.

"Try to fool me, will you, you yellow cur. Think I don't know where a yellow rogue always betrays himself? Keep your face as smooth as you want to, you can't hide that pulse. Now come inside, you who call yourself Soto. You were Nodo in Dutch Pete's gin dive in Banjermasin the last time I saw you. I want to ask you a few questions about the man whose throat was slit on the night you cleared out. Ah! That made the pulse nearly jump through the skin, didn't it? I've got you, Nodo, you murdering dog. You'll come through with what I want to know to-night, or you'll never see another dawn. Now come."

And with that Plummer hauled the now limp Jap through the open window into the gloom of the room beyond.

6. The Sensation of Hollywood.

MR. SEXTON BLAKE, the famous London criminologist, lay in his large, beautifully furnished room at the Imperial Hotel in Los Angeles lazily approving the various fitments of the apartment, and remarking inwardly how decidedly superior in comfort the average American hotel bed-room is to what one finds in England.

There is no question but that the Americans have brought hotel efficiency to a point which is rarely to be found in Europe except among the very newest of the hotels de luxe, and Blake was the first to concede the superiority to our cousins across the Atlantic.

And, perhaps, nowhere in America outside of New York has money been spent more lavishly in this direction than in the city of Los Angeles, and the wealthy movie centre, Hollywood.

He was thus idly engaged when there came a tap at the door, and a moment later a floor waiter entered bearing his morning tray. Blake sat up, wishing the man a "good-morning," and at the same time finding he was decidedly thirsty for his tea.

The waiter was followed by a valet who brought in his clothes, which he had placed the night before within the space between the double doors with which his room was equipped, together with letters, some telegrams, and half a dozen morning papers.

Then followed the turning on of his bath in a bath-room that was the last word in modern luxury, after which Blake, clad in a thick, silk dress-gown of rather startling mixture of colours, settled down with his cigarette and correspondence.

But he was not fated to finish this morning ritual undisturbed. Scarcely had he ripped open the telegrams, which he found with one exception to be from London, than the desk telephone began to buzz. With a slight frown of annoyance he reached over and drew the instrument towards him. It was, he opined, probably Tinker ringing up to see at what time he would be down in the lounge.

Instead of his assistant's well-known voice, however, he heard, at the other end of the line, deep tones speaking in a strong nasal twang.

"Am I speaking with Mr. Sexton Blake?" was the query.

"Yes, I am Sexton Blake," answered Blake. "Who are you, please?"

"This is Peter J. Constant speaking, Mr. Blake. Maybe you have heard my name."

"Yes, Mr. Constant, I have heard your name in connection with the Cataline Fishing Club."

"I must see you at once, Mr. Blake. I am speaking from my apartment in the same hotel. May I come to your suite?"

"Y-yes, Mr. Constant—very well."

"Thank you. I shall be there in about five minutes."

Blake hung up the receiver, and, rising, made his way into the sitting-room of his suite. The place was flooded with the early morning sun, and here and there about the room were bowls of crimson and yellow flowers. It was more like the room in one's own home than a hotel apartment.

Placing his correspondence close at hand, Blake lighted a fresh cigarette and settled into an easy chair to await his coming visitor. He had said that he knew Peter J. Constant's name in connection with the Cataline Fishing Club; but he knew it also as the name of the multi-millionaire who had piled up many millions through the phenomenal growth of Los Angeles and Hollywood.

However, Blake did not see why he should voice that phase of his knowledge over the telephone. He was not at all impressed by the fact that the magnate should wish to see him on, apparently, some urgent matter, and he didn't intend that Constant should get any such ideas into his head.

The millionaire was prompt to the second; it was exactly five minutes later that there came a tap at the door, and the turning of the key as the floor waiter admitted the visitor. Blake cast a quick glance at the big, lumbering man who entered, classified him perfectly in those few moments, and then was greeting him easily.

It was perfectly obvious that Peter J. Constant was in a state of supreme agitation. His face was red and puffy as if he hadn't slept a wink all night; his clothes were rumpled, his linen mussy—hadn't been changed since the previous evening, thought Blake. And then, as the millionaire shook hands, Blake caught the strong whiff of brandy on his breath.

"Something very out of the ordinary has happened," he said to himself. "This man has received a severe shock, and he is keeping his nerves from jumping with brandy."

Peter J. Constant dropped into a chair and passed a hand across his brow.

"Mr. Blake," he broke out jerkily, "I have come to you because you were pointed out to me as you passed through the grill-room yesterday. I have read and heard a lot about you, and if ever a man needed your services I need them this morning. I am the victim of some sort of ghastly 'frame- up,' and I can't figure out just how the brick has been dropped."

"Before you tell me what is wrong, Mr. Constant, I should remind you that I am in Los Angeles on a special mission in connection with some British clients of mine. My work here is practically complete, and it is my intention to leave for San Francisco. If there is something in which you need the assistance of a private investigator, why don't you consult some local man in Los Angeles or Hollywood?"

"Because," came the stormy reply, "because I can't trust a darned one of 'em. If the job has been framed up against Peter J. Constant, then those who are behind it are shooting for big game. This bunch here would sell out their own mothers at a price. I tell you the position is terrible, and unless I can get someone to ferret out the truth I am going to spend a few years behind prison walls if I don't go to the electric chair for murder."

Blake was genuinely surprised. At first he thought the millionaire must have been the victim of some particularly subtle form of swindle; and the investigation of such a case at the moment held no interest for him. But murder—Peter J. Constant, the richest man on the Pacific coast, one of the most influential magnates in the whole of America to be in danger of arrest on a charge of murder—that was a very different proposition.

"Even now they may be after me," went on Constant, with a groan. "I came straight on here from the bungalow, and managed to elude them. There were certain papers and documents in the safe in my apartment here that I wanted to get hold of before the police began snooping round. But I may be arrested at any moment during the morning, so what I have to say must be said quickly. You must listen, Mr. Blake, and you must help me. I will pay any fee you demand, but I can't trust any of these local men. There is something going on underneath that is too deep for me. But I am innocent; I swear it. I no more killed Posani than did you!"

"Mr. Constant, I do not say that I will take your case, but I am prepared to listen to what you have to tell me. Pull yourself together. I take it that someone has been killed—murdered, and that his name is

Posani; that you are in danger of being arrested on the charge of murder. But this is all confused. I haven't the remotest idea who Posani is, nor why you should be accused of killing him. Unless you can give me a coherent story, you are only wasting your time and mine."

The millionaire pulled himself together. Lighting a strong cigar, he smoked in silence for a few minutes; then, turning to Blake, he began to speak with measurably more composure.

"You are a European, Mr. Blake, and therefore, I take it, you have heard of the famous French actress, Madame Vali Mata-Vali, the Bird of Paradise?"

Sexton Blake stiffened the veriest trifle in his low chair, and his eyes flickered with a sudden interest.

"The name is well known to me, Mr. Constant; also I have seen her dance in her most famous piece, the Jewel of Asia."

"Ah! Then you will know how beautiful she is?"

"I concede that without reserve. But just how does Vali Mata-Vali enter into this affair which has upset you so?"

"I will explain, for I must go back to two years ago in Paris to lead to what has brought me to see you this morning. It was in Paris when I was making a tour of Europe that I met her. I have—er—been married several times. In fact, it was just after my third divorce that I went to Europe. In Paris I was very deeply attracted by Madame Vali Mata-Vali, and made her several offers of marriage. She would have nothing to do with me, however, and I returned to Los Angeles. Some months ago I married again, the lady being the well-known film star, Sonia Vensky."

"I have also heard of her," murmured Blake.

Again the millionaire wiped his brow.

"Well, now things begin to get complicated. It was about ten days ago that I was at my little bungalow about twelve miles down the coast from Hollywood. I have always kept that place more or less for my own private use, although there has never been anything to prevent my wife coming if she wished. On this night, however, I was giving a stag party to some men friends. We played poker until dawn, and after an early breakfast the bunch motored back into Hollywood. I turned in, but was up at my usual hour, and it was then, when I walked out on to the veranda, that I saw a white yacht lying at anchor just a few hundred yards offshore, and almost directly opposite the bungalow.

"While I was breakfasting on the veranda I trained the glasses on the craft. She was a stranger to me, and I was interested because I did not know the name nor recognise the burgee she flew. Well, while I was thus engaged I saw a man and a woman strolling up and down the deck, and soon after I recognised the lady as none other but Madame Vali Mata-Vali."

He paused, but Blake made no comment. He was, however, growing more interested, for the last occasion on which he had come into contact with Vali Mata-Vali had been at her chateau at St. Cloud, on the outskirts of Paris, and those who have read the record of that affair know how cleverly she succeeded not only in eluding the French police on her own account, but in taking George Marsden Plummer with her as well.

"When I tell you that the sight of her roused all the interest I had felt in Paris, I am only telling the truth," proceeded Constant. "I am not posing as any paragon, Mr. Blake. Our ideas of marriage and divorce in this country may appear a little free and easy to British people, and we will let it go at that. It has never worried me, and when I got tired I usually found the lady was just as willing as I to sever the bond, providing the alimony was sufficient, which it was. Not that I had any idea up to that morning of divorcing my present wife. We had not been pulling too well together for some time, and for once in a way the cause of complaint lay more with me than with her.

"I had settled a big bunch of money on her, and I was having the pleasure of putting up very large sums for her to spend while a lounge lizard in the form of Paolo Posani, a film actor, and my wife's leading man in her new picture, was getting most of her society. I am no man's fool, and I am not blind. I could see that Posani was crazy about her, and I knew a show-down would have to come soon. I made this statement to my wife, and, I remember now, to several men friends. We discuss that sort of thing rather freely out here. That is where this killing of Posani puts the skids under me."

7.   The "Frame-up."

"PLEASE keep to essentials, Mr. Constant."

"I will, but I am terribly upset. Well, to get back to Madame Vali Mata-Vali. I went out to the yacht during that morning, and renewed our acquaintance. She received me kindly. With her was her cousin, who is also her director of affairs—a Spaniard by the name of Machado."

Blake made a note of that, but said nothing.

"I invited them to lunch at the bungalow, and they accepted. But on my return I knew I should have to say something about having been married since leaving her in Paris. So I sat down and wrote a note, which I despatched to the yacht before they came ashore. This left it open for her to change her plans if she wished. But she didn't. She came, and was even more charming to me than ever. I lost my head entirely, and to you, as my professional adviser, I don't mind owning that I immediately began to lay plans for cooking up a divorce from my present wife, so that the way would be clear to marry Madame Vali Mata-Vali.

"Complications arose at lunch, for, quite unexpectedly, my wife arrived at the bungalow, accompanied by Posani. I could see that she and Vali Mata-Vali took an instant dislike to each other. Soon after that my wife's jealousy was roused by the announcement that Vali Mata-Vali had come out to California in order to have a personal interview with Morris Schwarz, the biggest producer in Hollywood.

"It seems that Schwarz has offered her a contract to make three pictures under him, and it is known now that the figure named is the highest ever offered by any Hollywood producer. I am a shareholder to a considerable amount in the Schwarz company, and my wife didn't know that until a few days ago.

"She and Posani both act under Schwarz, and when she found I was a heavy shareholder she immediately accused me of having inspired the offer to Vali Mata-Vali in order to get her out to California.

"But I give my word I didn't know a thing about the offer until she told me at the bungalow. Of course, I couldn't make my wife believe that. At any rate, there was the very devil of a row, and since then I have scarcely seen her.

"I have seen a good deal of Madame Vali Mata-Vali. She has

30

taken a big house in Hollywood as it was necessary to send her yacht down to San Diego for some repairs to the engines. But I have been discreet, I can assure you. Well, in the meantime, my wife has been seen more than ever with Posani. It was becoming one of the biggest scandals in Hollywood, and, believe me, it takes something to make this bunch talk.

"I didn't care. I thought I was strong enough to snap my fingers at the lot of them. And I assure you my attraction to Madame Vali Mata-Vali was, and is, the biggest thing I have ever experienced in a pretty full life. I offered her anything she cared to ask for if she would marry me when I was divorced.

"She didn't say 'yes' and she didn't say 'no.' But two days ago she seemed to yield. I tried to persuade her to elope with me to Mexico. I own an island down in the Gulf of California which is in Mexican territory, and I knew if she came there with me, my present wife would soon file a petition for divorce.

"Now, you as an expert on international law, probably know just how tricky some of the clauses are in the Californian State Code. You may recall a recent domestic difference between a certain well-known film star and his wife in which, by using certain legal process, the wife succeeded in having an injunction served against every bit of property he held in this State—cash as well as investments—so that he couldn't touch a penny of it, and she, as the wife, applied to receive the full income from it?"

"Yes, I recall the case perfectly, and I am fully acquainted with that phase of Californian law."

"Then you will understand that I figured not to be caught the same way. For days past I have been working quietly cashing in on my investments. I am a director in a dozen different banks and trust companies in the State and a heavy depositor in several more, I didn't try to sell my land; that would have created comment and roused my wife's suspicions.

"What I did do was to arrange a lot of mortgages—some here and there, spreading them among half the banks and trust companies in the State. I always did keep a large part of my fortune in United States Government bearer bonds, so that by yesterday I had in cold cash and realisable documents not less than seventeen million dollars which I could carry away with me. Once I was across the Mexican border, my wife, who was playing her own game and would have handed my money over to Posani, could whistle for the rest.

"I went to see Madame Vali Mata-Vali yesterday morning, and told her what I had done. I offered her myself and my whole fortune and she agreed to elope with me."

"Did you tell her how much negotiable stuff you had collected for the journey?"

"Well, I said it was more than ten millions. It doesn't do to tell any woman all the truth."

Blake smiled faintly at the cynicism. As far as he could tell up to the moment, the whole business was none too savoury, and Peter J. Constant would not have succeeded in securing his attention for ten minutes no matter what size fee he offered had his trouble been only the matrimonial mix-up which he had certainly asked for.

But murder was a different matter entirely, and when the affair brought in that elusive and dangerous woman, Vali Mata-Vali, Sexton Blake was keen enough to know just what part she had played in the game. Besides, there was her director of affairs, the Spaniard, Senor Machado. Blake had a feeling that he should like to clap his eyes on that Spanish gentleman.

"And how much of those ten millions did you offer to Madame Vali Mata-Vali?"

"I didn't make a definite offer. I should have settled half at least on her once she became my wife."

"But not before?"

"I'd have given her a hundred thousand or so for knick-knacks, but no principal until the ring was on her finger. I wanted that woman so badly that I was prepared to go to a high limit, but I'm not such a fool as to sit into a game until I know how many cards each player holds."

"Quite so; and now—the murder."

"I have reached that. When I left Madame Vali Mata-Vali in Hollywood yesterday I had a lot to attend to. It was late afternoon when I reached my apartment here in the Imperial, and I set about at once to check up things."

"Let me interrupt for a moment. Your apartment here—is it a permanent place of abode?"

"Yes, I have a portion of the sixteenth floor. I am a shareholder in the hotel."

"I see. And does your present wife occupy this apartment at all?"

"Usually when she is in Los Angeles."

"Then I take it she has free access to it?"

"Of course."

"Proceed, please."

"Well, when I sat down at my desk I found a note from Posani asking me to meet him at my bungalow last evening as he wished to discuss important matters with me. I was on the point of tearing the thing up and letting the fellow go to the deuce—for he and my wife had both tackled me about the contract Schwarz had offered to the French woman—when I thought that it would be as well to have the showdown before I cleared out. So I decided to go.

"I motored out there before dinner, and, on reaching the bungalow, found Posani already arrived. I couldn't help but invite him to sit down with me, and when we reached the coffee and liqueurs he asked me to get on with what I wanted to say. This surprised me, for it was he who had told me he wished to discuss matters. I told him I was waiting to hear him first since he had asked me to meet him at the bungalow, and he then denied having written any such request. He added that he had only come because I had written asking him to do so.

"Well, I need not tell you I hadn't written him a word. So I saw then that there was some hanky-panky business going on. I put it down to my wife, and still think she worked the game in some way. I denied having asked him to come, and he called me a liar. I should say that we had both drunk a good deal during the meal, and, considering our positions, you can imagine we were both ripe for a quarrel."

Again the millionaire passed his hand over his brow.

"I remember up to then quite distinctly," he said thickly, after a pause. "But my last recollection is of Posani leaning over the table shouting at me and telling me that he knew I had double-crossed him and my wife, but that I shouldn't get anything out of it because he and my wife were going away together and that I could have nothing but the satisfaction of divorcing her. I seem to remember, too, that he said he should take good care, acting for my wife, that she got a good slice of my fortune, and then I can't remember anything else until—until the early hours of this morning.

"I must have fallen asleep or, at any rate, I was unconscious for some hours. It was grey dawn when I awoke, to find that I had been lying all night with my head among the glasses on the table. I had drunk a good deal of champagne and brandy, as I have admitted, though I didn't know I had taken enough to knock me cold like that. But it must have sent me out like a log even while I was talking to him; or I was doped.

"At any rate, I had a terrible head on me and my mouth tasted like sin. I staggered to my feet wondering what had become of my Japanese boy, Soto. I moved round the table towards the bell, and then I saw something lying on the floor.

"To my horror I found it was Posani cold and stiff. I kept my wits about me sufficiently to turn him over, and then I saw that he had been shot dead. There was a hole in his forehead exactly midway between his eyes.

"I hung on to the table trying to pull myself together. Something told me that this was going to be mighty bad for me, and when I looked round and saw, on the floor beside my own chair, an automatic pistol, something cold gripped my heart. I examined it. The magazine was almost full, and a loaded cartridge was in the breach. But on the carpet back of my chair was an empty cartridge case. It fitted the weapon—it was a rimmed automatic type of .32 calibre, and even a child would have deduced that it had been discharged from that weapon. But I had had no such pistol on me when I sat down, and, as far as I know, neither had Posani, although he might have. If I only knew what happened after things went black with me—"

"Leave that for the moment, Mr. Constant," put in Blake quietly. "What time was it, roughly, that you lost consciousness?"

"It would be something after nine— not many minutes."

"Besides you and Posani, who else was in the bungalow?"

"As far as I know only Soto, the Japanese house-boy."

"Had you dismissed him?"

"After he served the coffee and liqueurs I told him not to come until I rang for him. I didn't want him to overhear what passed between me and Posani."

"And when you recovered consciousness at dawn, after your discovery of Posani's body and the pistol, what did you do?"

"I drank a whisky-and-soda and rang for Soto."

"Was he long in coming?"

"Yes—about ten minutes. He said he had been in bed and asleep."

"And then?"

"I showed him the body. He was shocked. I suppose, for he began to mutter a lot of stuff in Japanese. I asked him to tell me just how we were seated and how things looked when he was last in the room, and what he told me coincided exactly with what I remembered."

"Did you ask him if he returned to the dining-room before going to bed?"

"Yes; he said that he did not intrude because I had told him not to do so unless I rang. He said he thought that my guest and I might have started playing cards."

"Um! By the way, Mr. Constant, you say you drank a good deal of champagne and brandy during dinner."

"Yes."

"Why, then, on waking and receiving this shock did you drink whisky instead of keeping to the same form of spirits you had been taking?"

"Because the brandy carafe was empty."

"Did you recollect finishing it off?"

"I can't remember; I have tried again and again to do so. But I must have been going it strong if I did."

"And then what?"

"I dismissed Soto to his quarters, telling him to keep his mouth shut until I told him he could speak. I wanted to think. My brain was clear enough then, and I knew it was going to prove a very ugly situation even for me. I wandered into the living-room, and then I got the second shock. I should have told you that I had placed practically all my negotiable securities in the safe at the bungalow, so as to have them handy for the getaway.

"We had arranged that the yacht was to come up from San Diego and lie off the bungalow waiting for us. Well, the first thing I saw was the door of the safe wide open, and it took me just about ten seconds to discover that the whole packet of bearer bonds and more than one million dollars in "yellowbacks" (banknotes) were gone. The safe had been cleaned from top to bottom."

"How had it been opened? Had an explosive been used?"

"No, the person who opened that safe was a master. The combination is one of the very latest, and yet whoever opened it did so by using the correct code turns."

"Would anyone besides yourself know the code?"

"No."

"Nor have access to a copy?"

The millionaire paused. Then:

"There is a copy in the safe in my apartment in this hotel. My wife could have seen that if she had managed to gain access to the safe there. It is an old one that is worked with a key. She might have got hold of that key without my knowing it."

"And then?"

"I knew that someone was trying to cook me to a frazzle. Whoever it was had secured the sinews of war as well. There were twelve millions in that safe, and you can do an awful lot in the way of bribery in this town with a bankroll of twelve millions behind you. I knew that I must get back here as quickly as possible. All the rest of my stuff was in the safe upstairs. I found it intact, and I have brought the whole lot down with me in this bag. There are letters and papers and other documents as well.

"The police must not lay their hands on this stuff, Mr. Blake. You must take care of everything for me. You are my only hope. I tell you there is a rotten frame-up against me, and it has been worked with only one hitch."

"You speak as if you had definite suspicions."

"I have."

"Then if I am to help you, you must tell me everything."

Peter J. Constant leaned forward and fixed his bloodshot eyes on the detective.

"My wife," he said hoarsely.

"Good heavens, man, do you think—"

"I'm certain of it. Listen, Mr. Blake! Posani said he did not write to me asking me to meet him at my bungalow. That was a lie. He and Sonia Vensky cooked that up between them. Then he said he had received a letter from me making the same request of him. Another lie, for I sent him nothing. It was a plant to get me out there alone with him. I'll bet she was hanging about all the time. What part Soto may have played in the game I don't know. But something went wrong somewhere. I was to be the victim. It is my body that should have been lying on the floor—not Posani's.

"What did I do after Posani started to blackguard me? I don't know. Was I doped and did someone else pull the trigger that was the cause of his death? Or did I, in some alcoholic fit of madness, succeed in getting the gun away from him? Did I pull the trigger? No, sir. You can't tell me I could do a thing like that and not remember a single thing about it.

"But Posani was killed instead of me. Did Sonia Vensky do the job? Or did the Jap? Or did someone else who knew Posani was going to be there? He had lots of enemies who would bump him off quick enough. He has caused more domestic rows than any other person in Hollywood. But I was framed all right, and cold reason tells me it points to me as being the murderer of Paolo Posani."

"What did you do before leaving the bungalow?"

"Nothing more than I have said. I knew I must get away as quickly as possible. I had to get hold of the bonds and money I had left here and fix up my story to tell the police. And here is how I know it was a frame-up. Just as I was on the point of leaving the bungalow the telephone rang. I sent Soto to answer it. It was the Hollywood police at the other end of the wire. They wanted to know if everything was all right at the bungalow—said they had received a telephone message from some unknown person telling them there was trouble out at my place. I signalled to Soto to tell them to come out, and then I made myself scarce.

"It was no use trying to cover the thing up any longer. I knew it was hopeless to try to get away after someone had 'phoned the police. That was my wife again. She figured on having the police arrive on the scene and finding me there with the dead body. That is why I believe she was somewhere about the bungalow the whole time.

"She would know that things had gone wrong—that her precious Posani had been shot instead of me. And it must have been she who got away with the stuff in the safe."

"If that were so, then wouldn't she know that some other person had killed Posani?"

"She might; and she might even have had a hand in that. She may have wanted to get rid of Posani. All she really cares about is money, and she may have decided to make a clean sweep of things last night. What I don't understand is why I wasn't killed as well while I lay helpless."

Blake shook his head.

"Your theory is too confused, Mr. Constant. It won't hold water unless the Jap had a hand in it. In that case—"

But before Blake could finish his remark there came a heavy pounding at the door. There was something so definite and menacing about that hammering that Peter J. Constant blanched.

"The police!" he whispered. "Here, Mr. Blake, take this bunch of stuff! You must stand by me now! Look up my attorney, James Farquhar, in the Globe building. He will work with you. You can get permission to come and see me, but, for the sake of justice if nothing else, clear me of this terrible suspicion. I did not kill Posani, and if they can hang it on to me, they will put me in St. Quentin (the huge Californian State prison) for the rest of my days!"

In that moment Blake felt genuinely sorry for the man. He had brought most of this trouble on himself by his own disregard for the laws of Society. But Blake felt that the man was telling the truth when he denied having killed Paolo Posani.

He believed with Constant that the latter had stumbled into some deep and subtle frame-up, which would victimise him as well as strip him of most of his millions. There was a deep challenge in that which called to the hunting instinct in Sexton Blake, and, swiftly, he made his decision.

"Give me the stuff!" he whispered, while the hammering on the door recommenced and harsh voices called upon him to open. "I'll see your attorney and do what I can."

He grabbed the huge pile of papers and a leather portfolio, which the millionaire gave him with shaking hands; then, in a few swift steps, Blake crossed to the cold fireplace and deftly pushed the mass up the chimney. Next moment his voice rang out cold and level.

"Steady at that door! What do you take this room for?"

Striding to it, he turned the handle and opened it half-way. Outside he found three men crowded against it, heavy-set men in blue suits, who were obviously plain-clothes police. A little way down the hall was the floor waiter, shaking in his shoes.

"Well," snapped Blake, "who are you, and what the deuce do you mean by kicking up such a row on my door?"

One of the men made to push his shoulder into the room, but in a flash he went stumbling across the corridor as Blake gave him a hefty straight-arm.

"You come in here when you are asked!" he rasped. "I asked you what you wanted. My name is Sexton Blake, and these are my private apartments. If you have nothing to say, then stop making such a row!"

With that he made to close the door, but one of the men got his foot inside.

"We know you are Sexton Blake," he said surlily. "We don't want you, but we want Mr. Peter J. Constant, who was seen to enter these rooms."

"Why on earth didn't you say so civilly?" returned Blake. "If you have business with Mr. Constant, I have no doubt you can see him; but you will stand right there until he comes!"

By this time, the millionaire, his face like chalk, had risen. He crossed the room, and his tone held a forced bravado as he asked jocularly:

"Hallo, boys! What's all the row? What do you want of me?"

The three plain-clothes men shifted a little uneasily. After all, this man they had come to arrest was the multimillionaire, Peter J. Constant, a political as well as a money force in the United States. They didn't know just how things might go, and they knew millions could do an awful lot. Therefore, the spokesman was civil enough as he answered:

"Why—er—the chief would like a few words with you, Mr. Constant."

"All right! Do you want me to go along with you?"

"He said to ask you to do so."

"Right!" Then he turned to Blake, giving him a long, meaning look before holding out his hand. "Well, good-bye, Mr. Blake. Don't forget to buy those shares I recommended."

And with that Peter J. Constant went off under quiet, but none the less effective, arrest, to be accused of the murder of Paolo Posani.

8.   Blake Suspects Vali Mata-Vali.

NEEDLESS to say, the arrest of the multi-millionaire, Peter J. Constant, on a charge of murder threw Hollywood and Los Angeles into a perfect furore.

Special editions of the papers were in the streets within an hour of the arrest, and every copy was snatched up eagerly. It had been common gossip in Hollywood that everything was not right between Constant and Sonia Vensky.

The name of Paolo Posani had been freely mentioned in connection with the affair, and, from the imaginative reports that made up most of the first newspaper stories, it certainly looked as if the reporters had already tried and convicted Constant of the crime.

They made a terribly strong case against him.

In some way they had got hold of the fact that Posani had gone to the bungalow at Constant's request to talk things over. It was quite easy to build up on that base what must have happened. A row would naturally follow, and Constant, feeling fairly secure in the role of the injured husband, with all his millions and influence to back him, had committed the deed, as he had intended carrying it out when he had written to Posani.

"Is it to go out to the world that money and influence can flout justice in Hollywood?" demanded one emotional reporter of the yellow press.

"Because J. Constant is a multimillionaire, is he not to be subject to the same law as the poor man? Is this poor woman, one of the brightest stars in the Hollywood constellation, to be the victim of such a scandal as this because a jealous husband runs amok? Is Paolo Posani, one of the most popular of the movie colony in Hollywood, to go to his death for the crime of having played lead to this millionaire's wife?"

And so on.

The rest of the papers were more discreet. Aside from the fact that Posani had been one of the best-hated men in Hollywood it was difficult to picture Sonia Vensky in the role of the outraged wife. Her association with Posani had been too blatant for that. And, despite his peccadilloes, Peter J. Constant was well liked.

Instead of dwelling on the emotional phase of the affair, they concentrated mostly on the fact that Mr. Sexton Blake, the famous

British criminologist who was visiting Los Angeles, had taken charge of the case on behalf of Mr. Peter J. Constant, and they followed up with interested speculations as to how this British sleuthhound would measure up against the American detectives.

Before lunch-time Blake found his room besieged in the corridor and by 'phone. He settled the latter nuisance by the simple expedient of disconnection, and he outwitted the mob of reporters by nipping through his sitting-room window on to the fire escape and climbing down two floors to Tinker's room, which was directly beneath his own.

In that way he and Tinker (the latter completely mystified as to why Blake had appeared through his window, and was on the run like any criminal) managed to slip out of the hotel by a basement exit, and, hailing a taxi, drove at once to the Globe Building.

Blake thought it advisable to lose no time in getting in touch with Constant's attorney, James Farquhar, and handing over to him the enormous quantity of bonds and cash which the millionaire had entrusted to him.

On the way there, he gave Tinker a brief outline of what had happened just before in his sitting-room. Tinker, utterly chagrined that he should have missed such an unforeseen development, was all agog to get full particulars, and when Blake mentioned that in some way their old acquaintance, Vali Mata-Vali, seemed to be mixed up in the affair, Tinker could restrain himself no longer.

"I'll bet anything that Plummer is not far off, then," he said excitedly. "They were as thick as the thieves they are, in Paris, guv'nor, and if she is here, G. M. P. must be with her. I'll eat my hat if he hasn't had a hand in the killing of this dago! And twelve millions in bearer bonds and cash! That would be candy from home for Plummer! Don't you think so, guv'nor? Or do you think Mr. Constant did the job?"

"I didn't say Plummer was with Vali Mata-Vali. But there is with her a Spanish gentleman who rejoices in the name of Machado. I think we shall have to have a look at that scion of old Spain. As for Peter J. Constant, I do not for a moment think he is guilty of murder. If I did, I should not have agreed to accept the case. I must confess that the actions of everyone concerned are unsavoury to a degree but we are not concerned with their morals. We are out to ferret out just what sort of a 'frame-up' Constant has been the victim of, for I agree with him that he has been framed. And a word of warning: These American reporters are the very devil at digging themselves in. You may find one under your bed or hiding in your bath-room when you go back. But shoot them out with a gun, if need be. At any pressure, do not say a single word for publication."

"They'll find the Sphinx has moved from Egypt to Hollywood," responded Tinker, with a grin. "Gee! I'm glad this came up before to-morrow, guv'nor. It looks like a bit of excitement ahead for us."

If he had known just what lay ahead, he might not have been so keen on tackling the case, but neither he nor Blake could foresee that.

They found James Farquhar in his private room, in a large suite of offices on the twenty-fifth floor of the Globe skyscraper. He had not kept them waiting a moment. On the contrary, when his clerk brought Blake's name into him, he gave instructions that the visitors were to be ushered in immediately, and since every clerk in the main offices knew that the famous British detective was already retained in the sensational Constant Bungalow Case— as it became known—they cast deeply interested looks at the detective and his assistant when it was whispered that this was the great sleuth.

James Farquhar, a Scotsman born, who had come to California as a young man, greeted them warmly. On his desk was every extra paper he had been able to secure, and at sight of the big portfolio and brown-paper parcel which Blake carried, his eyes glinted, for Peter J. Constant had found means to communicate with him, and advised him that he had handed everything into Blake's care.

"I have been rather expecting you, Mr. Blake," he said, as he drew two chairs forward. "I heard from Mr. Constant about an hour ago. I am naturally deeply shocked to learn of this charge which has been laid against him, but I am glad that you happened to be there. You may take it that I shall do all in my power to be of assistance, although I am afraid I shall prove most useful in the legal end of it. As for the ferreting out of the truth and the securing of evidence with which to buttress up the defence, that must lie with you. I may say now that I shall give you and hope to receive complete confidence. I know, perhaps, more than any other man about Peter Constant's private affairs. I have handled his business for years, and his private affairs as well."

"I am glad you have cleared the way at once, Mr. Farquhar. It would be useless for me to try and help Mr. Constant otherwise. I will say now that I believe there have been very deep forces at play in this business, and it is not going to be easy to uncover them."

"We shall get no help from the police."

"But we shall get justice, I hope." The attorney smiled.

"The situation here may not be quite clear to you, Mr. Blake. I do not say that a judge and jury would not give Mr. Constant a square deal. But he is not going to find that the police of either Los Angeles or Hollywood will go out of their way to accommodate him."

"May I ask why?"

"I will explain. Unlike the system of appointing police in England and Scotland, which is mainly under the central government, the police forces of the cities in America are local, and entirely political plums. Unfortunately for Mr. Constant, he is a very strong Republican in politics, and last year an overwhelming Democratic ticket was elected in both Los Angeles and Hollywood. Ergo, he is not persona grata with the present people in power for all his influence, and a lot of his money was arrayed against them. It would tickle them no end to pin such a spectacular thing as a murder on to him, even if they did not finally succeed in sending him to St. Quentin.

"They would never get him into the electric chair, even if he were found guilty. He is too popular throughout the State and the governor is his personal friend. But a terrific lot can be done through legal quibble in America. We shall pull every string we can in order to delay his coming to trial. Whether we can get him out on bail I don't know yet. But we can expect strong opposition and all sorts of injunctions to tie up his estate, so he can't make use of it in his defence. I fancy his wife, Sonia Vensky, will make use of that weapon.

"The whole affair is a muddle to me. I know that he intended clearing out soon, and I arranged several heavy mortgages for him on most of his real estate. He told me that a large portion of his negotiable stuff had been stolen when Palo Posani was murdered, but that he had entrusted some money and bonds to you. I hope there is a substantial amount, for we shall need it."

Blake smiled as he laid the bundle and portfolio on the desk.

"I cannot say for certain, Mr. Farquhar, but I am under the impression that I have here something in the neighbourhood of five million dollars in bonds and cash. They should provide the sinews of war."

The attorney rubbed his hands in satisfaction.

"Thank Heaven he managed to reach you before the police arrived, Mr. Blake! This is splendid. I had not dared to hope that we should have such a fund. We can do much with five millions. And now, will you tell me, please, what you can of this extraordinary affair. What part has Sonia Vensky played in it?"

"I will tell you in a moment. But first I want you to understand clearly, Mr. Farquhar, that I have taken this case on my own terms. I believe Mr. Constant to be innocent of the murder of Paola Posani, therefore I am going to do my best to clear him of that charge. But that is not all. I understand that something in the neighbourhood of twelve million dollars in bearer bonds and cash were taken from the safe in the bungalow at the time of the crime. I am out to retrieve those millions as well."

The attorney's eyes glinted with admiration, then he shook his head slowly.

"You can count on me to the last shot, Mr. Blake, but it is going to be the toughest proposition ever tackled in Hollywood to recover those missing millions."

"We shall see. And now, Mr. Farquhar, this is the tale I had from Mr. Peter J. Constant."

Forthwith, Blake began, and gave the attorney a resume of the story which Peter Constant had related to him in his sitting-room at the Imperial. He had said nothing to the millionaire about his previous knowledge of Vali Mata-Vali, but to Farquhar he gave an outline of the case in which he and Tinker had run her and George Marsden Plummer to earth in Paris.

"So you will understand why," he added. "I cannot help but think there is far more in this than even Constant suspects. He hasn't the shadow of a doubt about Vali Mata-Vali. To him she is just the beautiful, famous, and wealthy actress he met in Paris. To me she is something very different. It is impossible to make a guess as to what part Sonia Vensky played in this business. Nor can we theorise as to what Posani may have had in his mind when he went to the bungalow. Those letters—Constant is emphatic that he did not write one to Posani. Did Posani receive one? If he did, then it was a forgery, and who was the forger? Among these papers I have given you we shall find the letter which Constant received, and which Posani denied having written. Was that a lie, or is it a forgery? If so, then someone who was very interested in getting the two together arranged it by a double forgery."

"By thunder, Mr. Blake, but I see how your mind is working. This gets more and come complicated each moment. That man Plummer—I have heard of him. He is one of the most dangerous criminals at large. If he is with Vali Mata-Vali, as you suspect, then we can look for anything—anything!"

"But that doesn't explain Sonia Vensky's position, nor that of the Japanese house-boy," responded Blake drily. "One thing is certain— Sonia Vensky would never work hand-in-hand with Vali Mata-Vali. No woman would join forces with another woman who was not only her rival in the same profession, but was stealing her husband and his money as well."

"You are certainly right there. It is the first law of human nature."

"Of the female of this species, at any rate."

"What do you suggest as the first step? I shall, of course, make immediate application for bail, but I expect they will keep me hung up on that for days."

"That must be attended to, of course. There are quite a number of things I wish to do. I want to pay a visit first, however, to the bungalow where the crime was committed. I take it the body is still there, and you, I suppose, can get police permission?"

"Certainly!"

"It will be necessary for me to be presented to the police as the authorised detective in charge of Peter Constant's case. I can bring certain high influence to bear myself if there is any trouble on that score."

"That won't be necessary. I can arrange it. The district attorney will grant me every facility. He is perfectly square."

"Good! Then I shall want to pay a brief visit to Sonia Vensky. I understand from the papers that she has locked herself in the Hollywood house and refused to see anyone. But she must see us."

"She will not refuse me. In fact, she has already telephoned to me asking me what I am doing."

"Well, I shouldn't mention my name until we reach the house. And, on my own initiative, I shall pay a visit to the bungalow which is at present occupied by Vali Mata-Vali. I want to have a few words with that lady, although I don't suppose the interview will yield much.

Also I want to have a squint at Senor Machado."

"That sounds a pretty useful programme to begin with."

"It is just that—a beginning. And before we go out to the bungalow I think it would be well if you made arrangements that on some pretext the yacht Thetis, which is now lying in dock at San Diego undergoing repairs to her engines, should not be allowed to leave American waters for the time being. The port authorities can detain her on some technicality."

"That will be easy enough."

"Then if you will identify me to the local police, I think it would be as well if we motored out to the bungalow while the ground there is still fresh."

Thus it was that, half an hour later, after leaving police headquarters, where Blake was introduced in his official capacity, and was certainly received with every courtesy—being given a special permit that allowed him every privilege he could have asked for— they were on their way to the Constant bungalow.

At the other end there was waiting for Blake the third shock in this sensational case he had tackled, but it was not until he stepped on to the veranda that he found what it was to be.

9. Blake Recognises Soto, the Japanese.

THE Constant bungalow, some twelve miles out of Hollywood, was like a good many others which had been built as a pied-a-terre along that stretch of beautiful coast. It was close to the sea, in extensive, wooded grounds which made it quite invisible from the Los Angeles road that ran all the way down through San Diego and on over the Mexican border to Tia Juana—the one-time collection of adobe huts in dust and mesquite, which became a boom place of racing and drink at the time prohibition was enacted on the statutes of the American constitution.

The road was superb, and were it not that his mind was engrossed in the problem before him, Blake would have revelled in the wonderful air coming down from the mighty hills that towered away to the east until they ranged on into the grandeur of the Rockies.

But his mind was like a well-oiled machine that day. He was turning over and over in his mind the story that Peter J. Constant had told him. In his uprush of fear and emotion the multi-millionaire had advanced half a dozen half-baked theories as to how the murder might have been committed, but even a trivial test of those had been sufficient for Blake to discard them as untenable.

Of one thing he felt convinced— either Peter J. Constant was guiltless of the killing, or, if he had done the deed, it had been when his brain was completely dominated by alcohol or some drug. It was difficult for Blake to conceive of such a seasoned drinker as Constant drifting into such a state of alcoholic aberration to enable him to carry out so many actions as the finding of a pistol, the deliberate shooting of a man, and, after that, the cunning robbery of his own safe. In the first place, if the crime had been committed by him in such a state, what was Posani doing while his host was getting the weapon?

It wasn't likely that he would sit quietly by while Constant rose to do such a thing, and then would be quiescent while the millionaire shot him down. The theory that it could have been done in a maze of alcoholic insanity was definitely discarded by Blake long before they reached the bungalow.

Then again came the recollection of the notes to which Constant had referred. He maintained positively that he had not sent any invitation to Posani, yet equally emphatic was he that he had received such a note from the Italian, and before leaving Farquhar's office they had come upon such a document, though they had not had time to give it a close examination.

Assuming that Constant had not deliberately planned the murder of Posani, then had the latter cooked up some scheme to kill the millionaire? Had he written to Constant to make the appointment, and then when he got on the scene maintained that he had come there because he had received a letter from Constant? If so, then what had caused his plans to miscarry? And how did it come that he was the victim instead of being the murderer?

Constant had not referred to any struggle. All his story amounted to when it was boiled down was that he and Posani had met at the bungalow; he had gone there because Posani had written asking him for a private interview. Posani had gone there—by his statement—because he had received a letter from Constant asking him to meet him.

There had been an angry discussion, but beyond that Constant could not remember what had happened. He had passed through a blank period of several hours, and then at dawn had awoke to find that he had been apparently asleep with his head among the dishes, and a few moments later had discovered Posani body on the floor.

The weapon had been lying on the rug beside his—Constant's—chair as if he had done the shooting and it had fallen from nerveless fingers. On the face of it the business looked condemning for Constant.

But if his story were true, how had the safe been opened? It had been done with a proper understanding of the code, or someone had possessed a most uncanny knowledge of safe-breaking. Constant said that his wife, Sonia Vensky, had access to his rooms at the Imperial, where she might have become possessed of the code, a copy of which was in his desk there.

There was ample reason for believing that Sonia Vensky was on very bad terms with her husband, but that did not presuppose that she hated him sufficiently to plan his murder. It needed brains of no mean order to lay out such a cunning scheme as one might construct round the affair.

For instance, supposing it were she who had written both notes—if Posani had actually received one—and had counted on a desperate row following, then what? Things might fall according to her plans, and a killing might ensue. But there were so many factors of chance in this that Blake could hardly accept it as a possibility, though he by no means eliminated her from his suspicions.

He figured that it was far more tenable as a theory that she and Posani had planned the deed, that Posani had never received any note from Constant, that in some way things had gone wrong, and that he had been the victim, while Sonia Vensky, who may have been hidden on the scene all the time, had grabbed the twelve millions in bonds and cash, and knowing that Posani was now counted out, had made herself scarce for her own safety.

In that event, then, she could only have done all this if the Jap servant had been her accomplice.

Once again this Oriental entered into Blake's thoughts. And now as he pondered still further possibilities he could not forget that for some days before the death Peter J. Constant had made himself conspicuous by his attentions to Vali Mata-Vali. To the world at large Vali Mata-Vali was just a French actress who had won fame and wealth in Europe.

Her coming to California but made her one more of the long procession of actors and actresses, authors and scenario writers who had been lured to Hollywood by the immense prizes to be won there, where money flowed as nowhere else in the world.

But to Sexton Blake she loomed as a very different star. He knew that she had thrown over all her contracts not so very long ago in order to embark upon one of the most daring criminal coups that had ever been attempted in Europe. She had deliberately chosen as her partner George Marsden Plummer, the most ruthless and daring criminal at large.

Between them the pair had brought to bear so much criminal pressure that it had exercised the Paris Surete more than any case for a long time, and it had even brought Sexton Blake into it. Therefore, was it possible, Blake asked himself, that Vali Mata-Vali had had no hand in this mysterious affair?

Constant had freely confessed to Blake that he had been planning to run away with the actress. He had acknowledged the realising of most of his negotiable investments, and had "planted" bonds and cash to the tune of something like twelve millions in the safe at the bungalow. Would Vali Mata-Vali be unaware of this? Certainly not; she would know to a fine degree just how much Constant was bringing with him.

And certainly twelve millions was a stake high enough to lure the most blasé crook, not to speak of the other five million dollars in bonds and notes which the millionaire had placed in his safe at the Imperial.

Further, there was the person who acted as Vali Mata-Vali's "director." Blake was not a little suspicious of this individual. It was quite on the cards that Senor Machado was none other than Plummer, and it didn't take any intricate deduction to reach that conclusion. But would Vali Mata-Vali and Plummer cook up such an affair as this, when the money would have been completely at their mercy within a few days?

Constant had at least been perfectly honest in acknowledging his intentions to Blake, and it was more because of this frankness that Blake had taken the case—plus, of course, his belief in the millionaire's innocence—than for any other reason.

And even if Plummer and Vali Mata-Vali had planned such a killing, what could be their motive? Did they know about the twelve millions being in the safe? And did they possess enough information about the triangle formed by Constant, his wife, and Posani to plan such a thing, just in order to get at the safe and throw such suspicion upon Constant that he would be unable to move hand or foot, while they made a clean get-away.

Blake knew that Plummer was quite capable of such a coup, and under his experienced fingers the safe at the bungalow would not present insuperable obstacles. But if this were so, then again it could only have been carried out if the Jap butler had been overcome or was an accomplice.

Whichever way Blake's mind worked it brought him back each time to the Oriental, and by the time they drove in at the gates of the bungalow—where a burly policeman was on duty—he was more anxious than ever to give the "once-over" to the house-boy.

Farquhar left the car parked in the shade of a wide-spreading clump of scarlet hibiscus that had had its origin on the slopes above Honolulu in the Hawaiian Islands. Then they proceeded on foot to the veranda.

Passing round by the side they mounted the steps, finding the inevitable wire screen door in front with the french windows wide open, but similarly protected by hinged screens that could be thrown open at will.

Lounging on the veranda was a plain-clothes man from Hollywood. He knew Farquhar by sight and nodded, but imposed a bulky form between the attorney and his two companions until Farquhar had produced a pass from the chief of police in Hollywood which gave them complete freedom of movement.

The constable cast a curious eye at Blake and Tinker as they followed Farquhar into the living-room, where the undersized figure of the Jap suddenly appeared.

"So that's the guy I've heard so much about?" was the muttered comment of the plain-clothes man. "Sexton Blake, the London flash detective. Well, all I've got to say is, that he's been overrated. He might be all right in dear old London, where it's always raining, but he'll find he's nothing but a jitney with a busted spring out here. And, anyway, what the gazabo expects to find I don't know. This job is pinned on to Peter J. Constant, and buttoned up so close there isn't a strait-jacket could fit any tighter. He'd better take that bony chin of his back to Piccadilly and give it an airing."

While this sprig of the Hollywood police was thus soliloquising the object of his thoughts was standing in the cool gloom of the living-room apparently interested in the colour scheme of the walls, while Farquhar interrogated the Jap house-boy. But already Blake had taken in the Oriental in one swift glance, and while there was absolutely nothing to reveal, the result of his scrutiny there was a considerable element of excitement within him, for it was the second time within less than a fortnight that this same Japanese, who called himself Soto in California, had been recognised as a yellow man, who, some considerable time before, had been "boy" in Dutch Pete's gin-joint in Banjermasin in the Dutch East Indies, some twelve thousand miles on the other side of the earth.

Nor was Blake's the only eye that had seen something familiar about the Jap. Tinker had also found his memory stirred, but he could not remember where he might have seen the Jap before. Blake's assistant was less experienced in discerning the baffling difference in the great mass of yellow faces of a certain type, and had come to the conclusion that the one who stood before him was similar in appearance to another he had seen during some of his peregrinations about the globe.

But had Blake mentioned a certain occasion when they had drifted into Dutch Pete's, following a gruelling chase after their man half through the southern jungles of Borneo, Tinker would have placed the fellow quickly enough.

As for Soto, not by the flicker of an eyelash did he betray whether or not he recognised Blake. His face was that of a graven image as he politely informed Farquhar that he could not give him permission to go over the bungalow as it was in the possession of the police; but that a police detective with two men was in the diningroom, and that his permission would have to be obtained.

"Which is the way to the diningroom?" asked Farquhar curtly.

For the bare fraction of a second the Jap's eyes passed across Blake's gaze, but it was just as if it were the mere curiosity of the man to take in the other visitors, for immediately he was again looking at the attorney as his low, smooth voice answered:

"Just across the hall, sir. I will show you."

He lifted a pair of magnificent Navajo blanket curtains as he spoke and stood aside while they passed out. Then, with a word of apology, he overtook them and lifted another pair of curtains, which allowed them to pause on the sumptuously appointed diningroom where three men, obviously of the police, but dressed in plain grey business suits, were standing by the table of beautiful Spanish mahogany in deep converse.

All three turned sharply at the sound, and one of them, the chief of the trio Blake quickly surmised, recognised Farquhar, for he called him by name.

"You, Mr. Farquhar—what are you doing out here?"

The attorney stepped into the room, smiling genially as he did so.

"Good-afternoon, Morrison. Let me introduce to you my friend, Mr. Sexton Blake of London; and this young man is his assistant, Tinker. I fancy you have heard of Mr. Blake."

The detective bent a pair of very shrewd and piercing grey eyes on the Britisher. Then he put out a hand that gave Blake's a firm grip. He extended the same welcome to Tinker, and followed by naming his two assistants, Corbett and Heaver. After that his eyes went back to the attorney.

"Well, Mr. Farquhar, what can I do for you? I take it, from the fact that Mr. Blake has come along with you, that you are interested in the little dust-up that took place here last night. I shall be glad to extend every possible courtesy to Mr. Blake, but I am afraid I can't give you the run of the place without a word from the chief."

"That's all right, Morrison, I've got a full permit for myself and my two friends. We went to police headquarters before we came out."

While he was speaking Farquhar was taking out the permit he had received, and, after a glance at that comprehensive paper, Morrison nodded.

"That's enough for me. Glad to hear what you think of it, Mr. Blake. It might be a little different from the type of case you get in England. They call us a 'gunman' country, and this sure is a 'gun' job if ever there was one. But you won't find much mystery here. It is a dead 'open and shut.' Old Pete Constant flew a little too high this time, and all his millions won't keep him out of St. Quentin. He sure picked a bad time to pull off this stunt. There is such a howl about the notorious scandals of Hollywood that the public are yelling out for a conviction, and, believe me, Pete Constant is going to be the example. But as a straight 'open and shut' bit of gun-work, you may find it interesting."

Blake thanked him.

"It is only chance that I am here," he said in a casual way. "I should have been on my way to-day to San Francisco had it not been that Mr. Constant asked me to take up an inquiry into the case on his behalf. Therefore, I feel I ought to tell you that both Mr. Farquhar and I are out to find anything we can which will assist in the defence."

Morrison laughed. Blake had already decided that, of all the police officials, uniformed or otherwise, he had met in Hollywood or Los Angeles, he liked Morrison best. There was something keen and open about the man that appealed to him, and he had a feeling that, despite the fact of his being out to gather any possible evidence to wreck the police case, he would not be obstructed by Morrison. As a matter of fact, before Blake had finished with the notorious Constant Bungalow Case, he and Morrison were destined to become warm friends—a friendship built on a mutual respect.

"You're welcome to go as far as you like, Mr. Blake. If you can dig up anything that will appear favourable to old Peter J., then good luck to you! I ain't anxious to see the poor old guy railroaded, even if he was a high-flyer. And I'd like to see you at work. You won't mind if I watch you, I suppose? No offence meant, but some of the reports I have read about your cases seem to give the impression that you are a wizard, and can pick up a clue out of thin air, as the saying goes. If you can pick up anything here that will help old Peter J., then I'll tell the world you are all they say, and more."

He made the personal reference in such a good-humoured way that it was impossible to take offence. Blake knew that he would need this man's good will if he were to get a fair run at the bungalow, so he smiled in a way that he could make very charming when he chose.

"I am afraid reports have greatly overrated my ability," he said lightly. "I have had a lot of luck at times; and you know what newspaper reporters are in the 'dead' season. But I appreciate your offer, I can assure you; and perhaps there are one or two things we can dig up in Mr. Constant's favour."

"Huh! I guess not! But go ahead, by all means. Where would you like to begin?"

"With the body, If you don't mind."

"All right. It's all the same to me. The dago is laid out on the bed next door. You won't need to spend long there. The doctor has already made his examination. That poor gink was drilled clean between the eyes by a thirty-eight calibre bullet, and it wasn't any case of suicide. There isn't a spot of powder on the skin, and the gun was found on the floor beside the chair which Constant had occupied. But come on, and I'll show you."

And, without making any comment, Blake started forward, feeling that at last he was getting to grips—inwardly determined, too, that if the faintest shadow of a clue existed that would help Peter J. Constant, he would dig them up despite the cocksureness of the police that the millionaire was already as good as convicted.

10. American and British Methods.

ASIDE from the fact that the body of the man on the bed was the central factor round which this grim drama centred, Blake was interested in studying the still features of him who had been such a furore in the screen world. He was not one of those superior persons who sniffed at the "movies" as a pernicious form of entertainment, for he knew from experience that some very beautiful photographic work and fine acting was to be seen on the silver screen.

And, while he had never seen Posani in action, so to say, he knew from remarks Tinker had let drop that the man was an excellent actor in some type of exotic stuff, even though he had become the idol of emotional women.

A single glance was sufficient to show that death had been instantaneous. The hand that had pulled the trigger of the weapon which caused Paolo Posani to plunge into the unknown, had been steady as a rock, and the aim had been perfect. A pair of compasses could not have marked that hole between the eyes more perfectly centred than it was.

Could it be, then, Blake asked himself, that this clean drilling had been done by a man who was in the throes of alcoholic dementia?

He did not prolong the examination. There was nothing for which he was seeking to be learned from those full lips that now were closed in grim death. It was but a few moments after he had first bent over the form that he straightened up, signifying that he had seen enough. They all trooped back into the hall, and then once more entered the dining-room. Here the hush that had held them in the room of death was broken.

"Well, what next?" asked Morrison, taking out his cigar-case and offering it.

Blake pinched the end of the Manila and placed it between strong, white teeth. He accepted a light, and blew an appreciative puff or two into the air before responding:

"I have read a considerable amount of the methods of crime detection in America, Mr. Morrison, and, through my New York agent, Bryant Kennedy, I have seen a certain amount, aside from the lone hand my assistant and I have played on occasion in your great country. I have always understood that it was a prime factor in your system to make a careful reconstruction of the crime as you believed conditions to exist when it was committed. Have you done that in this case?"

"Well, now, do you tell me that Bryant Kennedy is your New York agent, Mr. Blake!" exclaimed Morrison, not answering Blake's question. "Why, that boy had his early training under me in New York!"

"Are you, then, the John Morrison of whom he often speaks?" asked Blake, in genuine surprise.

"I sure am! I heard he had struck out in a private line of his own, but I didn't know he had hitched up with you. How is he doing?"

"He is a second Pinkerton," was Blake's immediate and sincere statement. "He has gone far, but he will go farther."

This discovery established an immediate bond between them. The American detective had been perfectly friendly before, but now he seemed more than ever anxious to do all he could to assist Blake, which, considering that it was up to him to collect evidence which would make a water tight case against Peter J. Constant, was rather decent of him. In fact, Blake had already found it a pleasant change to come up against a man who was keen, able, and yet modest—a striking contrast to some of the American police officials and detectives with whom he had sometimes worked.

"So you think we ought to have made a reconstruction of the crime," proceeded the American. "Well," and he grinned frankly, "I was waiting for that question. We have done so. Look here."

As he spoke he moved his position so that Blake could walk round and see the floor on a side of the table which, until now, had been invisible to him. There was there, as on the other side of the mahogany, a fine Turkish rug about three feet wide by six or seven in length. If one were sitting at that side of the board one's chair would be on this rug, though now, if there had been a chair, it had been removed.

An irregular line, drawn in heavy white chalk, caused Blake to bend lower. It was roughly the form of a kidney bean, part of the outline being on the rug and part on the floor. In area it would cover as much as—say, the huddled from of an adult, and, indeed, it leaped at once to Blake's mind that this chalked line showed the position in which the body had been found.

He expressed this thought to Morrison, while the attorney and Tinker bent closer to follow what he was doing. The two detectives who were in attendance upon Morrison had moved back a little, but they were closely watching the Britisher at work. Morrison confirmed Blake's suggestion with a nod.

"Quite right. The body was lying just in that way. Here you will see where the feet were drawn up; this curve here represents the line of the back, and this bulge in the line marks how one arm was thrust out. The head is indicated by this mound in the line at this end, and where it goes in with a deep sweep shows the bend in the front of the body." Suddenly he turned to the smaller of his two assistants. "Here you, Corbett, lie down and show Mr. Blake just how we found the body."

The man stepped forward, and, taking care not to obliterate any of the chalk marking, got himself into a position that almost fitted the rough outline on the rug and hardwood floor. From that, Blake could reconstruct an almost exact picture of how Posani's body must have lain when he had fallen from his chair, and he made a private note to the effect that if this did represent the position—that is, if the body had not been deliberately placed in such a position, then it would appear almost certain that the man must have fallen from the chair after being shot, for it was strongly indicative of how a dead man would slump from his seat to the floor with no nerve or muscle power to control his movements.

When he had expressed himself as satisfied, and had turned to Tinker to tell him to make careful notes of this, he found Morrison already busy bringing forward two chairs—one an armchair, and the other a straight-backed chair, and both fashioned in beautiful mahogany.

"Now I am going to show you how we figure the thing was pulled off," he announced. "Here is the armchair placed just where Constant was sitting. We have obtained a full description of this bit from the Jap servant as he saw them when he was last in the room. And here, right over this bit of purple flower in the rug, is where the pistol was found. You can see— But wait. Sit down here, Heaver, and re-enact the scene with Corbett. Now, Mr. Blake," he continued, when the two detectives were seated as he had directed, "Heaver here is supposed to be Peter J. Constant. Put your arm over the chair arm, Heaver. That's the ticket. Now take this pistol—yes, this is the actual weapon that was used in the job, Mr. Blake; you can examine it later. Now lean forward a little, Heaver, and let it fall from your hand.

There! Do you see, Mr. Blake, how it has fallen? It is almost as it was found. You take the other attitude, Corbett. Lean forward a little more; make as if you were having a heated argument with Heaver. Good! Hold that pose. I'll have you two birds on the movies yet. Now pick up the pistol, Heaver; level it—there! Now slump a bit and let it fall again. Good! First rate!

"Now, Mr. Blake, you have just seen how Peter J. Constant drilled Posani. What do you think of it? And I've even gone further. I have had ordinary photographs taken of the body before it was moved, of this scene you have just witnessed, and a movie bit of Corbett and Heaver acting the part. I will give you a run through of that as soon as it is ready, which will be some time this evening. Do you think now that we are as up-to-date as your Scotland Yard?"

Blake nodded his approval. There was no doubt that Morrison had considered every possibility, and certainly Scotland Yard had nothing more finished in the way of procedure than this. But there was this one difference which Blake could not help but note— like every other police official and detective connected with the affair, Morrison had started on accepted premises that Peter J. Constant was guilty of shooting Posani while the two sat at that table.

Scotland Yard might have suspicions of a man, but they would weigh every shred of evidence, and follow up each slender clue as far as possible before preparing their case, and not until the man was actually standing his trial would they permit themselves to accuse him of whatever deed it was that had been committed. And Sexton Blake was there to discover, if it existed, some slender thread which would shatter this cut and dried evidence which had been jotted down by officials who, in their minds, had already convicted Constant of the murder.

"I certainly must admit your efficiency," was Blake's remark. "It is doubly interesting to me as showing how the minds of two races so closely akin as the British and true American— which your name shows you to be— can be influenced by two or three or more generations of environment."

"How do you mean?"

Morrison's voice was puzzled.

Blake smiled slightly.

"I mean in the different way we approach a thing."

"Do you mean in the reconstruction of the crime I have just

shown you?"

"Yes."

"Well, how else would one approach it? Would you do so in a different way?"

"I think so."

"But how?"

"Do you wish me to show you?"

"I certainly do, if you will take the trouble."

"It will be no trouble; in fact, I should like to do so."

"Well, shoot the works, Mr. Blake. I'd like to see in what other way you can show me how old Peter J. killed Posani."

"I didn't suggest that I would show you that. I said I would use different methods to reconstruct the crime. When I have done that I may be able better to tell you if the man who sat in this armchair did the shooting or not."

Morrison laughed good-naturedly and his two assistants smiled in unison.

"That's a good one, Mr. Blake. Whether Constant did the shooting or not—why, man, it is a dead cert! No one else could have done it."

Blake did not respond to the sally.

"Shall I proceed?" he asked quietly.

"Go the limit. I am more than interested now, but you won't be able to hang that shooting on to anyone but Peter J. Constant."

"In order to make the reconstruction as I think I should like to make it, it will be necessary for me to make use of the houseboy for a little. Have I your permission?"

"Certainly; the place is yours for the purpose."

Blake rang the bell, and when the Jap showed up a few moments later he beckoned him to approach.

"You set the table for dinner last evening?" he asked abruptly.

"Yes, sir."

"You remember just how you laid it— what dishes you put on and where you placed them?"

The Jap hesitated for such a brief part of a moment, that only Blake could be sure that he was not ready to answer "yes" or "no." The fact of the matter was the Jap was puzzled to know what this man was getting at. And Blake knew it, for he had intended to catch him before he could make up some story to meet the questions.

"Yes, sir."

"Then start now and lay the table just as you laid it last evening. Do not forget a single item—do you understand? It is most important for the sake of the man who was killed that everything should be exactly as it was. Do you understand?"

"Yes, sir."

Blake then turned to the others.

"Shall we go out on to the piazza while he is getting it ready?" he asked.

They all assented, and for the next ten minutes or so they sat in the deep veranda rocking-chairs gazing out at the blue, limpid Pacific, discussing the case as it was known so far, Blake drawing out Morrison to talk while the detective was in an expansive mood, but inwardly thinking of how the yacht Thetis had lain just offshore some ten days before.

Tinker was picking up every word Morrison said, for he knew that Blake was about to try his own methods in a desperate attempt to drag out of the mass of condemning evidence which loomed against Peter J. Constant, some item, no matter how trivial, which would give him the lead he was seeking. Tinker knew it might well fail completely, and he wanted to be primed with every statement Morrison made in case it might come in useful at a critical moment.

As for Farquhar, he was content, as he had been ever since arriving at the bungalow, just to listen and mark all that was said. He knew that Blake's trained mind would grasp anything that protruded, so to say, and his job was to assemble later whatever evidence Blake might be able to pass on to him.

By the time the Jap came to the french window to call them back to the dining-room, Morrison had finished his resume of the affair. He had dwelt on every phase, going into such a profusion of details that they heard Constant's history from the time he first drifted into Los Angeles and made his first start in real estate speculation through the medium of a game of draw-poker.

Then, as they returned to the diningroom, they caught sight of an array of gleaming silver and glass and snowy-white napery that rested in pleasing contrast against the dull finish of the single great mahogany panel that formed the top of the table. There was no table-cloth, Constant evidently having favoured the then prevailing fashion of small mats under plates and dishes.

Sexton Blake paused and surveyed the arrangement with a critical eye. The Japanese houseboy was standing at one side, his eyes fixed on Blake. His face was utterly expressionless, and his attitude was that of a servant waiting for a word of approval. But Blake did not give it. Instead, he walked a little closer to the table, and, after a further look, turned suddenly to the Jap.

"Mr. Posani drank whisky last evening," he said abruptly.

"Yes, sir."

"Was it in a decanter?"

"Yes, sir."

"It is not on the table."

"I bring, sir. I forget."

With that the Jap hastened to the big mahogany buffet, and lifted up a heavy, cut-glass decanter which was about half full of an amber liquid. He placed it on a small, hemstitched linen mat on the right of the place he had laid where the unfortunate Italian had sat.

Blake walked round, lifted out the stopper, sniffed the contents, replaced the stopper and set the carafe back on the table without comment. It was whisky all right, and, if his nostrils were any good, of a good quality. But now once more he turned to the Jap.

"Your master, Mr. Constant, drank brandy. Why haven't you put it on the table?"

"I forget, sir; I get."

"Wait a moment. I told you to set the table exactly as it had been laid last evening, didn't I?"

"Yes, sir."

"And here, to my knowledge, are two things forgotten. What else have you neglected?"

"Nothing more, sir. I think sir want just dishes placed—I not know sir want drink on table when no food."

It sounded reasonable enough, so Blake let it go. But he frowned when Soto brought a perfectly empty cut-glass carafe and placed it close to where he had laid the place on the other side. Picking up the decanter he held it towards the window.

"Is this the carafe used by your master?"

"Yes, sir."

"It contained the brandy he drank last evening?"

"Yes, sir."

"It is quite empty. Did he drain it?"

"Yes, sir; he drink all."

Blake removed the glass stopper and sniffed. There was but a faint suggestion of spirits. He knew in a moment that the carafe had been recently washed.

"You have washed it since last evening," he said curtly.

"I—yes, sir, I wash. It dirty, so Soto wash."

Morrison was growing interested in this passage. It had not occurred to him to do other than give a careful but none the less passing glance at the carafe. He had regarded it as only an unimportant factor in the case—nothing more than the receptacle which had held the liquor which the guilty man had drunk.

But this Britisher seemed to regard it in a different light, and he had already discovered that the Jap had washed it since Constant had used it. Just what was Blake getting at, he asked himself.

Blake set the carafe down and stepped back.

"Do I understand that Mr. Constant drained this carafe while at the table?" he asked in a casual tone.

"Yes, sir; he drink all."

"Did you supply him with any more?"

"No, sir, I gone to bed."

"Then how do you know he drained it at the table?"

The Jap was startled despite himself.

"I—I find him empty," he stammered.

"But why should you think it was Mr. Constant who drained it? Why should you make such a statement? Is it because you are willing to state that your master shot his guest?"

"I—I not know anything, sir," responded the Jap, who now had himself in hand. "I find decanter empty—I wash him—I know master drink brandy —I think he finish decanter."

"All right. You may go—to the back quarters."

The Jap withdrew. Blake did not enlighten the others as to why he had laid such stress on the two decanters. But now he motioned to Tinker to seat himself in the place which had been occupied by Posani, and, sitting down where Constant had been seated, he turned to Morrison.

"If I may have the pistol for a few moments, Mr. Morrison, I shall make my demonstration."

And Morrison, far more intrigued than he would have cared to acknowledge, handed over the weapon, following which Sexton

Blake and Tinker got to work on a reconstruction of the shooting of Paolo Posani, which was to have considerable bearing on the final solution of the Constant Bungalow Case.

It was Sexton Blake at his best, and he hadn't been in action five minutes before the American detective knew he was watching the work of a master.

11.   The Scene at the Bungalow.

TINKER needed no coaching in the part he had to play. He had performed in a somewhat similar manner many a time in the past, and in this particular case he had already had from Blake a concise repetition of the story as it had been told to the detective by Peter J. Constant.

More than that Tinker had kept his ears and eyes well open since he had arrived at the bungalow, and had marked well how Morrison had described the crime to Blake.

Therefore, he assumed at once a natural pose, relaxing in his chair, with one elbow on the table and leaning forward a little, a truculent expression on his face as if he were prepared to contest strongly some statement Blake was making.

While he held his pose thus, Blake also leaned forward, and for a few moments the two went through a silent pantomime, as if each were working himself into a high pitch of anger.

Then, suddenly, Blake jerked his hand downwards, producing the pistol, which he had placed in the right-hand side pocket of his coat. His next action levelled the weapon at his vis-a-vis, and while he held it thus Tinker threw himself backwards as if he were trying to dodge an unexpected bullet.

"Watch, please," said Blake in low, clear tones that penetrated to the farthest corner of the room. "Get this movement, Mr. Morrison. I want to discuss it with you presently."

The American detective was leaning forward, missing nothing of the reenactment of the drama that was going on before him. Now he merely gave a grunt, which signified that he was taking in each detail, and, at a slight nod from Blake, Tinker allowed his body to slump to the floor. He fell to one side, hunched up over the irregularly drawn chalk line in a way that followed the outline in a remarkable degree.

Then Blake allowed the pistol to fall from his hand, which he was now holding over the arm of the chair. The weapon struck the soft pile of the rug with a dull thud, and remained just where it had fallen. Glancing down Blake saw that it was some three or four inches from the purple flower in the rug where it had lain before, but this, he knew, might be because the armchair had not been placed in exactly the same position by the Jap, or, in the length of his arm and that of Peter J. Constant—if it were from Constant's arm the pistol had

64

fallen.

Blake rose, and, walking round the table, looked down at Tinker. Then he beckoned to Morrison.

"You have seen our little reconstruction," he said quietly. "You can also see how my assistant has fallen. So similar is the attitude to that which you found Posani's body, so closely does the curve of his body follow the chalked line that I think we may take it without doubt that Posani did fall from his chair after he was shot and that the body was not intentionally placed there."

Morrison's brow's went up.

"You are not going to try to advance a theory of that sort, are you, Mr. Blake?"

"Not now," answered Blake dryly. "But in my efforts to discover some clue which will assist Mr. Constant, I cannot neglect anything. And I know now that Paolo Posani was not killed by the man who sat in that armchair."

Detective Morrison looked utterly incredulous; Farquhar moved forward with increased interest; Morrison's two assistants grinned and winked at each other.

"I am afraid you will have to put forward some pretty strong stuff to convince me of that," said Morrison, whose tone was thoroughly polite, but whose expression was one of disappointment that the British detective should try such "feeble" stuff on him.

"I'm going to prove it right now," was Blake's cool response. "Let us consider one or two things. The first is a return to the bed-room. I want you to make a fresh examination of the hole in Posani's forehead."

Greatly at a loss to understand what Blake was getting at, and with a suspicion that he was trying to put across a bluff, Morrison led the way in silence to the bed-room. The others, with the exception of Tinker, who maintained his hunched-up attitude on the floor, followed, and when they stood once more beside the still form, Blake very gently turned the body so Morrison could see the wound in the lower part of the skull at the back where the bullet had ploughed its way out.

"That is all I want you to look at," he said, in a hushed voice. "I noticed it the first time. Just take the line from where the bullet entered between the eyes and where it emerged. Have you got it?"

Morrison nodded in silence, and after a brief glance towards

Farquhar and the others, Blake re-arranged the body as it had been. Then he led the way back to the dining-room. Pausing once more beside the table, he turned to the American.

"You have seen the body, Mr. Morrison. How tall a man would you say Posani was?"

"I can tell you exactly, for the doctor took measurements. He was six feet and half an inch."

"Right; we shall accept that. I should have guessed a trifle less. And how tall would you estimate Peter J. Constant?"

Morrison winkled his eyes and pondered.

"About five ten or so," he hazarded.

"Wrong! He looks about that, but he is not more than five feet nine. I have stood beside him, and I am sure I am right. Now, have you ever noticed anything peculiar about Mr. Constant's build?"

"N-no, not particularly, except his bulk. He is a heavy man."

"Quite so. And what I have also noticed is that his legs are long in proportion to his torso. One doesn't notice that particularly owing to his bulk, but sitting down he shows it plainly."

Farquhar here broke in.

"You are right, Blake. I have often remarked that when he has been in my office."

"All right, I concede it," said Morrison. "But what about it?"

"That fact has considerable bearing on what I am going to say in order to maintain my claim that whoever sat in that chair could not have killed Posani while he was sitting, unless he had been at least six feet four or five, and long in the torso at that. It was a physical impossibility for Constant to do it if he were sitting down when the shot was fired."

"I'm a good listener," was Morrison's dry response.

Blake smiled good-naturedly.

"All right; now for the next bit. As they sat at the table, you will agree, I think, that Posani's head would be on a higher level than that of his host."

"Yes, I give you that."

"Recall, please, my action when I pretended to shoot Tinker. Did you notice that, even though I am considerably taller and longer in the torso than my assistant, my arm was at an angle that, had I actually shot him between the eyes, the bullet must have passed upwards after entering the skull?"

The American was showing no incredulity now. His every faculty was concentrated on following Blake's argument.

"Go on!" was all he said.

"Well, assuming that Posani was shot while he sat in that chair, across the table from Constant, the latter would have been compelled to rise to his feet in order to do the killing, for you must have noticed how, after entering between the eyes, the bullet that killed Posani took a downwards course, proving beyond the shadow of a doubt that the person who killed the Italian was standing, for in no other way could his arm have been so high and at such an angle as to direct that bullet as it travelled."

"Then Constant must have jumped to his feet!" countered Morrison quickly.

"I grant you that is a possible theory," responded Blake. "But now I am going to tell you why I do not believe that the bullet was fired at all by whoever sat in this armchair. Recall that wound again. I agree with you that it was not self-inflicted. It would be a most rare thing for a man to drill himself through the head in such a fashion with the bullet following that course. And besides, we may take it for granted that Posani did not come out here in order to blow his brains out, and, after killing himself do a physically impossible thing by hurling the weapon across the table to fall on the floor beside Constant's chair. No; he was murdered, and, in my opinion, the murderer stood behind those curtains just within the french windows that give from this room on to the side veranda."

"The deuce, you say! Impossible!"

"You may think so; I don't. Look here. If Constant shot Posani then he had to get to his feet. You have acknowledged that."

"Yes."

"Well, I know Constant is right-handed, for I have seen him use his hands. Therefore if he sprang up during a quarrel and whipped out that weapon, we may take it that Posani did not sit quietly in his seat while he was drilled. But even if Constant was quick enough to do all that before Posani could rise, then, if he shot with the right hand, the bullet would have followed still a different course, for the angle of aim would have been a little to the right, and therefore the bullet would have come out somewhere in the region of the skull that lies under the lobe of the right ear."

Morrison scratched his chin reflectively. Farquhar had an odd glint in his eyes. Morrison's two assistants were no longer exchanging grins and winks.

"Well?"

"The opposite would have been the case had Constant been left-handed."

"But where do you get the idea that the killing was done by someone who stood behind that curtain?"

"Because it is the only place affording complete cover sufficient for a human being in this room from which a bullet fired would come in a direct line, almost perfectly so, with the forehead of a person sitting in the chair which was occupied by Posani. Get up, please, Tinker, and sit down again."

While Tinker was obeying, Blake once more retrieved the pistol, and, walking to the heavy draperies by the french window, drew them across in front of him. Then, slowly, his arm showed while he drew back the curtain sufficiently to allow him to peer towards the table.

And, watching, the others could not help but see that, should he shoot as he was now holding the weapon, he would, if his aim were true, drill Tinker clean between the eyes; and from the slightly depressed angle of his arm the bullet would take a course similar to the hole that had been made in Posani's head.

Blake stepped out from behind the curtain and laid the pistol on the table. Then he drew out his own case of choice Partagas, and offered it. When the smoke was once more arising, he resumed:

"I have made this demonstration before the 'enemy,' as it were, in order that, should it come to a cross-examination in court, Mr. Farquhar and you will both be in a position to confirm what has taken place here this morning; for"—and Blake again smiled— "we shall now have to subpoena both you and these other two gentlemen as witnesses for the defence, I think."

Morrison was impressed, but not convinced.

"I'll own you have gone at the thing from an angle that hadn't occurred to me," he confessed. "But it will take a lot more than that to make any jury believe that Peter J. Constant did not do the shooting."

"I have shown only the skeleton of the defence which we shall build round this phase of it," responded Blake coolly. "I suppose if I were able to show reasonable grounds for the belief that Constant had been heavily drugged, you would consider my theory had been strengthened?"

"I sure would. But drugged! What do you mean?"

"You see, Mr. Morrison, I am going on a firm belief in the entire innocence of murder, or even attempted murder, on the part of my client. I accept his statement that he did not have any weapon on him at all, and had in no way planned the killing of Posani. I accept his statement that he had received a note, and that it was this which brought him to the bungalow last evening. Further, I think you will agree that, if he did tell the truth, and was lying asleep with his head among the dishes on the table during all those hours, until dawn, then it was either due to a very heavy dose of overdrinking of brandy, or else he was drugged. From dawn to now is something like eleven hours. If my suggestion should prove correct, then we should have to allow something like nineteen or twenty hours from the time he first began to absorb the drug until now."

"You mean the brandy was drugged?"

Blake shrugged.

"It was the liquid medium which would have been certain to convey it into his system, although I fancy even a laboratory test would show no traces of anything in the carafe now, for it has been washed this morning. At the same time I should take it as a favour if you would either have such a test made by the police analyst, or permit us to have it done."

"I cannot hand the carafe to you without consent from higher up, but I can do the other, and will see that it is attended to at once."

"Thank you. It is a pity that the houseboy was so efficient in his duties."

"You don't suspect him of anything, do you?"

"I have no definite suspicions of anyone—yet."

"But if that brandy was drugged, then it must have been done by someone who knew that Constant would drink it and that Posani would not touch it."

"Quite so; that is exactly what is in my mind."

But Morrison shook his head.

"It won't do, Mr. Blake. You'll have to show us something stronger than that to bolster up such a claim on behalf of old Peter J."

"I intend to do so," responded Blake calmly. "And now, if you have no objections, I should like to make a brief tour of the bungalow. I want to examine the safe and have a look at the grounds."

"Certainly. But will you excuse me if I don't come round with you? I want to get back to Hollywood. I'll take the carafe with me, and if there is anything at any time I can do I shall be glad to give you my time, Mr. Blake. We must get together and have a bite to eat one of these evenings. I want to talk about that lad, Bryant Kennedy."

Blake thanked him for his obvious wish to be friendly, and then, accompanied by Farquhar and Tinker, he moved into the living-room, where in one corner reposed the safe which had been looted of something like twelve million dollars worth of securities and cash.

But Blake did not proceed direct to the strong box. As he stood in the centre of the room gazing about him, his eyes happened to rest on the blue Pacific, which he could see through the wide-open french windows; and, out there, just drifting along slowly to an anchorage, was a beautiful white yacht, on the bow of which he could read the name Thetis,

12. Important Movements.

THE sight of the yacht was no little surprise to Blake. He had been given to understand that she was undergoing repairs at San Diego, and that she would not be permitted to leave Californian waters for the present. Then how did it come that she was about to cast anchor here opposite the Constant bungalow, where she had been lying on her first arrival?

It immediately occurred to Blake's mind to wonder just what motive Vali Mata-Vali might have in bringing the yacht along to this part of the coast, or, as he thought more likely—if the so-called Senor Machado was really George Marsden Plummer— what scheme was working in the master criminal's mind.

He pointed out the craft to Farquhar and Tinker, and, as he expected, the former put into words the questions which he had already asked himself. But Blake shook his head.

"You ought to be able to answer that better than I. You know how things are wangled out here. We shall probably find that strings have been pulled in Los Angeles, but why is she here? That is what concerns us more urgently than the fact of her being here. There it goes! See—the anchor!"

And even as Blake spoke, they could see the flukes disappearing beneath the surface. Blake continued on his way to where the safe stood, but his examination there did not take him long. It was perfectly plain, after he had brought into play his powerful pocket glass, that the safe had not been forced by tools or had the blowpipe been used. It was, obviously, the work of someone who had either known the secret of the combination, or had succeeded in solving it, either with nimble wits and a good ear, or with the assistance of a microphone.

The fact remained that it stood as a clean job, and it was but natural that there should come to Blake's mind the words Peter J. Constant had used about his wife having access to his desk in the suite at the Imperial Hotel.

Blake had just finished when Morrison entered the room. He was drawing on a pair of gloves, and was followed by Corbett and Heaver.

"I'm just on my way back to Hollywood. Mr. Blake—is there anything I can do for you before I go?"

Blake shook his head.

"No thanks—unless you can tell me how it comes that the yacht which is lying out there, and which, I understand, belongs to Madame Vali Mata-Vali, the actress, is back in the anchorage she occupied on her first arrival in Californian waters. I understood that she was laid up at San Diego and would remain there."

Morrison swung round sharply and showed distinct amazement at the sight.

"Well, holy smoke!" he ejaculated. "That's got me beat. You can search me, Mr. Blake. Her appearance here is as big a surprise to me as to you. I don't know how it comes about. I thought she'd be in San Diego for some time yet. I don't know just who put through the request, but someone certainly asked that she should be held at San Diego until after the Constant trial."

"Mr. Farquhar had a hand in that, but he certainly hasn't had anything to do with her departure from San Diego. However, I don't suppose it makes much difference where she is."

Then in a more casual tone:

"By the way, I understand the lady is in residence in a villa in Hollywood which she has taken."

"Yes, I understand she is going to do some work for Schwarz of the Cosmos Film Corporation. But you can't pin anything on to her, Mr. Blake," added Morrison humorously, "you will need something different than you have put forward to-day to help old Peter J."

"You may be right. But please don't forget to get that carafe analysed."

"I'll put it in hand to-day. Give me a call on the 'phone any time tomorrow, or look me up, and I'll let you have the result."

"Thank you. When will the body be moved?"

"This afternoon. It will be taken into Hollywood to Posani's own bungalow. There will be an inquest tomorrow, and as soon as we hear from the relatives in Italy we shall make the funeral arrangements. They may want it embalmed and sent across the Atlantic."

A few moments later Morrison and his two men took their departure, leaving only the plain-clothes man on the veranda in charge until the body should be moved.

Blake understood that the Japanese houseboy would then be left alone in care until the affair was wound up. He was pondering deeply on various phases of the matter, but principally about the unexpected showing up of the yacht while he, Farquhar and Tinker strolled through the grounds, and it was not until they were well out of sight of the house that he spoke.

"To my mind," he said, as if he were resuming a subject they had already been discussing, "the most important item so far is to clear up, if possible, the question of whether Constant was doped or not."

"How on earth can we do that except by accepting or discarding his own statement?"

"Do you know Constant's medical adviser?"

"Of course—Dr. Greatorex."

"Are you friendly?"

"Quite; we play golf together."

"I take it you could make application for certain medical tests to be made in connection with the prisoner?"

"Of course; they can't refuse that. And, besides, we may have him out on bail by this evening. I shall see about it the moment I get back."

"Well, a pathological test might show what we are trying to discover. It is now nineteen or twenty hours since the dope would have begun to enter his system if he was drugged; allow another five or six hours before the test could be made, and we go over the twenty-four. But a pathological test might reveal a trace, and a stomach pump is a mighty useful thing at times."

The attorney's brow cleared, and he shot an admiring glance at Blake.

"Scott! But you forget nothing, Mr. Blake! I should never have thought of that. I'll get hold of Greatorex the minute I get back to Hollywood, and get him busy on that stunt."

"Good! Tell him it must be of the most thorough nature. I didn't mention to Morrison that we might do that —It wasn't necessary, and we might be able to spring a surprise on the prosecution if we can get any definite trace of a drug. I think that, for the moment, we have seen all there is here to interest us. We may as well all go back to Hollywood and attend to various details there. I am rather keen to know if Sonia Vensky has been making any further effort to get in touch with you. There is the question of money; if she hasn't had any of what was taken from this safe, then she must be wondering about funds, for we certainly have what Constant had placed in the safe at the Imperial. Further, I want to pay a visit."

"May I ask to whom?"

"To Madame Vali Mata-Vali. I am more than curious about that yacht, and I think the solution lies there."

"Then have you definite suspicions of her and the man with her?"

Blake gave Farquhar a straight eye.

"There has been a deep mixture of cross-purposes at work in this business, Farquhar. What part Posani was playing we don't know yet. But there is a strong possibility that he and Sonia Vensky were plotting some devil's scheme against Constant. I hope to prove that. With the man dead, and Constant arrested, the woman may break in some direction. We can but wait.

"Aside from that, I believe an even more sinister element has entered into the business. You have asked me if I have any definite suspicions of Vali Mata-Vali and George Marsden Plummer; I would suspect them of anything, for they are capable of going the extreme criminal limit. But I will tell you even more why I believe there has been a deep play of cross-purposes, and this brings the Japanese house-boy into the case. That Jap in the bungalow was at one time kicking round a gin dive in Banjermasin, in Borneo, in the Dutch East Indies.

"I recognised him the moment I laid eyes on him. And as soon as we get back to Hollywood, Tinker is returning here in a suitable disguise. I want that Jap watched; I cannot get it out of my mind that the return of the yacht will bring forth some sort of move on his part. So let's get going."

. .   .   .   .

More than once that day had Sonia Vensky been in Sexton Blake's mind, and, could Blake but have kept secret surveillance upon her in the privacy of her luxurious boudoir at just about the time he was returning from the Constant bungalow to Hollywood he would have found cause for even deeper pondering.

Although it was getting on towards that hour in the afternoon when the film star usually was to be seen driving, and acknowledging with gracious smiles the greetings of those who were only too anxious to be on speaking terms with one who was not only a world-famous movie star, rich in her own right, and the wife of the multimillionaire to boot.

Hollywood had not made nearly as much malicious gossip about Sonia Vensky and Paolo Posani as they had about Peter J. Constant. And, for once in a way, gossip was right. Paolo Posani was the constant attendant upon Sonia Vensky, and was, as rumoured, deeply in love with her.

But Sonia Vensky had not one grain of love in her for the Italian, for the simple reason that she had no room in that scheming mind of hers for anyone but herself.

Her marriage to Constant had been a purely commercial proposition as far as she was concerned. But she had figured a little too optimistically regarding the millionaire. He had not been as easy to handle in a financial way as she had calculated.

It is true that he had settled a very substantial sum of money upon her at the time of their marriage, but that was but a small portion of what Sonia Vensky had decided should come into her possession from the millions she knew he had locked away. He meant just that to her—nothing else. For never since the world began to go round had it given birth to a more shrewish, more inveterate money-grubber than the one-time dancer in a low-class Polish cafe, Sonia Vensky.

Never did Jew in old Frankfort reach out grasping fingers with more avid greed than she! Never did a Shylock whine for his pound of flesh with more penetrating wail than Sonia Vensky nagged at Peter J. Constant for more and more and still more money. That much, out of decent shame, had the millionaire kept even from Sexton Blake.

She was a money vampire. She would have sold her soul, if she had possessed one, for money. Her deposits were scattered among a dozen different banks with the care of a miser, and also so that none should know the exact extent of her wealth.

Her friendship with Paolo Posani had been coldly calculated with an eye on using him when opportunity offered. Vali Mata-Vali had thrown over everything at a moment when she was at the very pinnacle of fame as an actress and dancer in order to embark upon a career of crime with George Marsden Plummer.

But it was not the lure of easy gain that had drawn Vail Mata-Vali into the game. Rather was it the excitement, and, after her first meeting with Plummer, a deep infatuation for that rogue.

But no man ever had held Sonia Vensky's interest, and none ever would. She had played Posani like a cat would play a mouse. The Italian had been as wax in her hands, and, on the night that he was killed, there had been between them an understanding—a pact which not one soul in all Hollywood or Los Angeles suspected with the exception of Sexton Blake. And it would need a deal of iron-clad proof before Blake or anyone else could nail down that suspicion into a certainty.

Nevertheless, at the hour when she usually drove abroad in her luxurious, imported Rolls-Royce, Sonia Vensky was locked in the privacy of her boudoir, invisible to even her most intimate friends. She had not been out of her private suite except once that day. This was a hurried visit she had paid to the local police headquarters in order to attempt to get an interview with her husband. But though she had sent in to him three different messages, Constant had been adamant in his refusal to see her.

She had returned then to her house, and the only communication she had had with the outside world was by means of the telephone and one visit which she received after her futile attempt to talk with Constant.

This visit was from a fashionable lawyer, Gutenburg by name. He was the attorney who acted in most of the hectic scandals which shook Hollywood from time to time, and was about as slick in the handling of a case as any man who ever entered a court. She had sent for him following several futile attempts to get hold of her husband's attorney, James Farquhar.

It will be recalled that she had succeeded in getting through to Farquhar on the telephone a short time before he and Sexton Blake drove out to the bungalow. But Farquhar had been extremely cautious in what he had said to her. He was acting altogether for her husband, and therefore had to give a certain amount of leeway to the wife. But she had failed utterly to get out of him any information as to what was happening with regard to Constant's money.

Farquhar had made a shrewd guess when he told Blake that Constant had been right in thinking she might make use of Californian law by having a quick injunction served to restrain any dealings by the prisoner with his own money, claiming the right to have a voice in the matter, she being concerned for his welfare as his legal wife.

Had she succeeded in doing this, she would have been in a strong position, and, while outwardly feigning to assist in her husband's defence, would have been able to transfer the bulk of the estate to her own control. This was but a precaution, for James Farquhar did not guess the vicious depth of purpose that was going on in the woman's mind.

But in addition to finding a blunt refusal from her husband at police headquarters, she had also received a hint that had made her frantic to learn the truth about what disposition had been made with Constant's money. Sonia Vensky knew that several millions had been placed by the millionaire in the safe at the bungalow. Peter J. Constant had not been far wrong in some of his apparently wild statements to Sexton Blake, for if things had gone as she had intended those millions would now have been in Sonia Vensky's possession.

Peter J. Constant, however, was wrong in thinking that she and Posani had planned a meeting at the bungalow that was to end in his—Constant's —murder. He was also wrong in thinking that Posani had lied to him when he had denied having sent any note.

Sonia Vensky had been trying for some time past to plan something that would give her possession of a big slice of Constant's fortune, and if he died in the process without risk to her, so much the better.

But while she was deeply involved in the affair of the night before, there were phases about it which were as much a mystery to her as to Constant himself, and not least of these was the Japanese house-boy.

That afternoon, as the sun sank in the west and night approached, Sonia Vensky felt a deep stirring of fear within her. Of Posani she thought scarcely at all, and when she did it was but to anathematise that poor wretch for having bungled matters badly, and to add a vicious curse upon him for allowing himself to be killed before accomplishing her purpose.

For, in the test which had come so opportunely—as she had thought—the Italian had been as wax in her hands. But something utterly strange had intervened, something so mysterious that it had struck a deep chill to the heart of the woman.

She felt that she was in a maze from which she could find no way of escape. There seemed to be revolving all about her vague forces which she could not grasp, but which she felt instinctively were menacing her safety. She was frantic to see the Japanese boy and question him about what had taken place at the bungalow. She had been there when Posani had been killed, and yet she knew not what hand had dealt out death to him.

She began to suspect Constant of having fooled both her and Posani until the moment came to strike. And she had a deadly fear that he had outbid her in buying the acquiescence and silence of the

Jap.

But when the lawyer, Gutenburg, arrived, she found fresh material to feed her terror. Gutenburg had learned about as much as anyone knew, and, having a shrewd idea that he could not possibly bring tears of wifely sorrow to the eyes of Sonia Vensky, he laid it before her bluntly.

What she learned was that Constant had realised on practically every bit of negotiable property he possessed. She knew that he had been gathering together a certain amount of money, and a mysterious message had been her source of knowledge about the millions that had been placed in the safe at the bungalow.

But since the murder she had begun to think that this message must have come from Constant himself, and had been but another sly play in the game he was "pulling " on her and Posani.

Gutenburg knocked that theory to shreds. She learned that what may have been placed in the safe at the bungalow, and which, if the open door was any indication, had been stolen, was by no means all that he had realised.

She knew only one other place where he would hide anything, and that was the safe in his suite at the Imperial Hotel. At this point she made up her mind that she would lose no time investigating there, for she had access to the place, and a key of the desk where she knew the key of the safe was kept in a secret drawer.

Then followed Gutenburg's blunt disclosure that Constant had been on the point of leaving the State in the company of the woman with whom his name had been coupled so frequently of late—Vali Mata-Vali. Sonia Vensky's eyes went red with rage as she listened.

A wild thought came to her that perhaps it was Vali Mata-Vali who had thought out this whole business—that she had planned so cunningly that the money had come to her while Peter J. Constant was in prison. Was it possible? she kept asking herself over and over, while she listened to the rest the lawyer had to say.

She retained him to act for her. She instructed him to use every trick he possessed, and to pull every political string in his power to find out what had become of Constant's millions.

"If there's anything in the safe at the Imperial I shall get it," she said. "But you must do everything! I care not what I pay!"

"It will cost money," he had assured her. "I stand in with the 'powers that be,' but the wheels must be greased, and Samuel

Gutenburg's sendees are worth money."

It galled her to the extreme to be compelled to draw on her own money to keep things going, but she was forced to do so; and then, when the suave lawyer was gone, smug in the knowledge that which ever way things went his pockets would be well lined, she waited for dusk. Under cover of that she motored in a closed saloon to Los Angeles, but when she finished her ransacking of the desk and safe there she knew that again she had been fooled.

From the suite at the Imperial she got on the 'phone to Gutenburg. She told him she had drawn a blank, and elicited from him that he was already busy on her behalf. He was able to tell her, too, that Posani's body had been taken to Hollywood from the bungalow, and the police withdrawn, leaving the Japanese houseboy as caretaker.

Her voice was on the verge of a tremble as she bade him keep in touch with her. Then she descended to the ground level, where she dismissed her saloon. She was afire with anxiety to get out to the bungalow and talk with Soto, who, at last, it seemed, was alone. But she would not even trust her chauffeur to know whither she was bound.

She walked round to a garage in a side street, where she paid a substantial deposit, and secured a small coupe of a well-known make, which she could drive herself. (This form of hiring is general throughout America.) Then she drove at a rapid pace out of Los Angeles until she came to the branching road that would take her to the bungalow.

The coupe flew like a shadow through the night, but it was not the only shape that sped out the road to the bungalow that same evening, for close enough behind so that her course could be followed, stole another car, at the wheel of which was Sexton Blake.

13.   Tinker's Movements at the Bungalow.

WHEN Blake made his disclosure to Farquhar and Tinker that he had recognised the Japanese houseboy, Soto, as having been employed in Dutch Pete's gin dive at Banjermasin, sudden enlightenment had come to Tinker. Again and again he had found something hauntingly familiar about the little yellow man, but, as has already been said, he had put it down to general race likeness. But when Blake mentioned Dutch Pete's, it all came back to him.

There was by no means as much coincidence as there might appear in the fact that the Jap had been recognised by Plummer as well. Dutch Pete's in Banjermasin is the general jumping-off place for all that part of the East Indies, as anyone knows who has been there.

It is as much the Café de la Paix of those myriad islands which lie between Java and the Philippines as the original café in Paris is the cross-roads of Europe. Everyone who drifts east of Singapore and gets off the beaten track, even a little way, eventually passes through Dutch Pete's joint.

Therefore there was nothing strange in Plummer being acquainted with the place, for, like a good many other adventurers who knock about the world, he had drifted up and down the China coast and among the islands of the eastern seas on many an occasion when Europe and America had been too hot to hold him.

Likewise, Sexton Blake and Tinker had found their footsteps taking them into and out of Dutch Pete's on some one of the numerous long chases they had had in overtaking a fleeing criminal.

And, with particular reference to Soto, there had been an incident that stuck out from the ordinary which had stamped the yellow man's face in Blake's mind. Now Tinker recalled the occasion, and with the realisation that this little yellow crook was planted here on the other side of the globe, came an understanding of a good deal of Blake's procedure at the bungalow which, until then, had puzzled him.

He understood perfectly in this new light why Blake should be anxious to discover something about how the Jap would conduct himself when the body was no longer in the bungalow, and all the police supervision had been removed.

It was in the dressing-room of Farquhar's large bungalow, which was situated among beautiful trees and shrubs in wide, secluded grounds, that he questioned Blake. Farquhar was a bachelor, and had

80

thought it better for the time being that Blake and Tinker should take up their quarters with him in order to avoid being pestered by reporters.

So, in an unobtrusive way, their luggage had been brought through from Los Angeles, and now Blake was sitting on the side of a couch in the dressing-room, advising while Tinker got into the disguise of a typical American household canvasser, of which tribe there is a large number in America.

"I knew that bloke's mug was familiar, guv'nor," he remarked, as he got into a pair of baggy trousers, "but I never fixed him properly. Fancy him being here in California! What was the name at Dutch Pete's—Nogo, wasn't it?"

"You are not far wrong, old son; it was Nodo!"

"Do you think he is mixed up in this business, sir? He was an awful little crook in those days."

"I don't think; I am almost certain that we could get the whole yarn from that close-mouthed little Jap if we could screw the truth out of him. He is a big factor in this case, Tinker; that is why I am so anxious for you to keep a close eye on him. That Jap was no more in bed at the time Posani was killed than I was on the scene of the murder!

"If that carafe of brandy was drugged, then it could only be through the Jap that the dope could be introduced into it. Either the person who planned that murder knew that Constant would drink practically nothing but brandy, or else he, or she, had to get the information from the Jap. In either case, the carafe had to pass through the yellow man's hands. And I shall be keenly interested to know if an analysis of any faint remains which may have stayed in the decanter, or a pathological test of the contents still to be found in Peter Constant's stomach, as well as his blood, will reveal any traces of a drug.

"Once we could prove that such had been administered, and actually identify what it was, our case would be much, much stronger. Still, despite the cocksureness of our genial friend Morrison, I am not at all hopeless."

"What about the yacht, guv'nor?"

Blake was thoughtful for a few moments.

"Frankly, Tinker, I am puzzled. There has been some hanky-panky there. By all rights, that yacht should still be under repair at

San Diego. But strings have been pulled by someone, and we find her released. Not only that, but she is again anchored in front of the Constant bungalow.

"Now, the persons most interested in the movements of the yacht are naturally those who arrived in her. That means Vali Mata-Vali and her so-called director, Senor Machado. Just how they, perfect strangers, could pull the necessary political strings to get the yacht released, I don't know; but anything is possible in this country of 'graft.'

"At any rate, it shows, to my mind, that Vali Mata-Vali and her 'director' are not idle. Nor can I get away from the suspicion that the presence of the yacht at that particular anchorage has some connection with the affair we are investigating. I cannot believe that Peter J. Constant has had any hand in her release. And, if not, then we must look to Vali Mata-Vali for an explanation."

"And Plummer?" added Tinker.

"Yes—and Plummer!"

"Do you think they had a hand in killing, Posani, guv'nor?"

"Honestly, I haven't got that far yet, Tinker. But if George Marsden Plummer is the pseudo-Spaniard, Senor Machado, and got wind of there being a large sum of money in the safe at the bungalow, it wouldn't take him long to cook up some sort of scheme to lay his hands on the stuff; and it wouldn't have to be millions to tempt him. But this affair is much deeper than that. There are several cross-purposes at work. I do believe that Plummer and Vali Mata-Vali have had a hand in it; to what extent we still must ascertain. But, by Constant's own confession, he had realised on several millions in order to elope with Vali Mata-Vali. Therefore, she knew he had the stuff in a negotiable form."

"But why should she pull off a major crime when all she had to do was to wait a bit and work an easier game, guv'nor?"

"There may have been difficulties over the presence of Plummer. Constant is no man's fool. He may have objected to an elopement which included 'Senor Machado' as one of the party. He wouldn't speak of that phase of it to me. But for some reason or other they may have thought it better to plan more deeply.

"That is all tentative theory, and we mustn't forget that Sonia Vensky may have played a considerable part in the business. In fact, so anxious am I to get a line on that lady that as soon as you get started for the bungalow I am going to pick up her trail. I am going to move along that line even before I tackle the subject of Mata-Vali. So you know what your job is; watch the Jap and be guided by what may eventuate."

"Right you are, guv'nor. I'll keep my 'peepers' on him once I get there. How do I go?"

"You are to take Farquhar's two-seater. You recall the side road I pointed out to you as we returned to Hollywood?"

"You mean that one close to the bungalow grounds with the thick trees along each side?"

"Yes."

"I can find it all right."

"Very well. Leave the car a little way up that lane. Farquhar says it is an old track that runs up the valley and is seldom used. But jam the two-seater well into one side. Then get into the bungalow grounds. The rest is up to you. If you are caught you can bring out your samples of brushes and bluff that you have lost your way."

"Right you are, sir," responded Tinker with a grin. "If I get caught I'll sell the Jap some brushes. I suppose the police will be well away?"

"You will find no one but the Jap there when you arrive."

Thus it was that, a little before dusk, Tinker reached the side road of which Blake had spoken. Already Blake was out in another car trying to pick up Sonia Vensky's trail, but Tinker didn't know that; nor, even if he had, would he have had any time to think about it. He was going to need all his wits for the job in hand.

He did not meet a soul as he moved along beneath the big cedarwoods that lined the main road. It was easy enough getting into the bungalow grounds, and as soon as he was over the stone wall which bounded it, he took at once to the undergrowth, working his way along in zig-zag fashion in a direction that he knew must eventually bring him within sight and hearing of the bungalow.

Every few moments Tinker would crouch and listen. Time after time he could hear nothing but the lazy wash of the sea on the sandy beach; and once, when the trees thinned out, he saw the riding light of a vessel that he knew must be the yacht. Then he was once more in among the undergrowth, and presently he caught a glimpse of a dim light which glowed through a drawn red curtain.

When he had crept nearer he found that this glow came from the back of the bungalow. It must be, he figured, in the secondary kitchen from which the serving was done, for he knew that, a little way removed from the main building, was the outer kitchen for the cooking and the quarters for any servants that might be employed. It looked as if the houseboy was in that room.

How to discover what he was up to— that was the problem. Just near the back of the bungalow was a large cottonwood tree from which it would have been an easy matter for Tinker to see into the room had the curtains not been drawn. But there was no chance of using that point of vantage now, so, with infinite precaution, he crept round to the side of the building.

He was forced to crawl almost up to the veranda before he could make out whether the windows there were open or closed. He found that they were closed, so, continuing on his way to the front, he investigated there. They, too, had been closed, and, he imagined, locked as well.

So, taking advantage of the bit of cover offered by shrubs, he made his way round the next corner to the side on which the dining-room looked. Here he felt a thrill of satisfaction, for, standing wide open, were the french windows that had been introduced as part of Blake's demonstration earlier in the day.

Tinker flattened himself to earth and lay listening. From over the water came the low "tinkle-tinkle" of some sort of stringed instrument accompanied by the murmur of a deep voice singing. It proved at least that the crew was up and about on the yacht, and in that still air was a warning to Tinker that even faint sounds would carry distinctly.

Then he thought he could make out a sort of shuffling sound within the bungalow, as if someone whose feet were clad in slippers was moving about. As far as he knew it could only be the Jap, so, determined to get a peep at the yellow man if possible, he crept along bit by bit until he was close to the low veranda.

It was a simple enough matter to crawl under the rail, and then, like a shadow, he stole across and disappeared through the open window into the darkness of the room beyond.

In his rubber-soled shoes he made scarcely a sound as he tiptoed across towards the door he remembered as leading out into the hall, taking good care to avoid the table which he knew stood almost in the centre of the room.

The curtains made a slight "swishing" sound as he parted them to steal through, causing him to flatten his body against the wall in the hall in order to see if the Jap's suspicions had been roused. But evidently the slight noise had not reached as far as the kitchen, for no one came to investigate.

Tinker continued his progress after a few minutes. As he drew still nearer to the bend of the passage which he knew must lead to the kitchen he could hear quite plainly the low "slushing" sound he had noticed when lying in the garden; and, accompanying it, an odd little murmur that sounded as if the Jap might be speaking to someone.

Tinker's hand went down to the side pocket of his coat where he had placed an automatic pistol for use in case of emergency. Satisfying himself that it was ready for quick work in case of need he moved on again, and now, as he reached the bend in the corridor and peered round the angle, he saw a thin crack of light shining against one wall. The door leading into the kitchen was slightly ajar.

It was not until he was almost directly opposite the door that Tinker saw why the shaft of light was shining through. It was due to no carelessness on the part of the person within the kitchen, but was due to the fact that the door was of the type that was hung on a double-action spring, permitting it to be pushed a-swing freely from either side. In this case, as so often happens with that type of spring hinge, there had been a certain amount of weakening in the force of the spring, with the result that the door did not hang true.

For that reason a thin line permitted the light to flow out into the passage, and it was to this chink that Tinker now applied his interested gaze—one eye serving to bring into focus a good portion of what lay on the other side.

It was, as he had thought, an inner serving kitchen, and the occupant was none other than the yellow man who called himself Soto in California, but had been known as Nodo in Banjermasin. The "slushing" noise which had attracted Tinker's attention was due to the fact that Soto was moving about the room, his feet clad in a pair of common type of Japanese slippers.

And the low murmur which had accompanied the sound was explained now by Tinker's discovery that the Jap was, apparently, singing! There was no other explanation of the queer sounds that were being emitted from his throat.

Had it not been such a strange, uncanny sort of sound in that place which had seen murder so recently, Tinker would have been inclined to find it humorous. Aside from a few occasions in Japan he had never heard a son of that country indulging in vocal exercises of this type, and the song, if so it could be called, was a most ludicrous bit of two-note monotony that seemed to have no beginning and no end, no verse and no chorus as it is understood in the West.

"Ki li sinto ee-ai-ka lo—seek! mum ee mo ee-ai-ka-lo—"

Just that it was on only the two notes, repeated over and over and over again, while the singer moved back and forth, back and forth across the room.

It was only now and then that Tinker could catch a glimpse of the Jap. He seemed, so far as Tinker could judge, to be parading up and down with his hands locked in front of him doing nothing but give voice to that monotonous drone.

And yet Tinker knew enough of the race to realise that Soto would not be doing this just to while away a lonely evening. There was some motive in it—something beyond what he could see.

As yet, however, he dared not risk pushing the door wider. He knew that as he walked in one direction those slit brown eyes would be in full line with the door, and the slightest move would become evident. Therefore, all Tinker could do was to stand and watch, wondering if the strange dirge was ever going to end.

It did—suddenly. Without warning the Jap's voice went up to a high treble pitch that is beyond the vocal scale of most Europeans. It hung there, then followed a jumble of strange sounds which culminated in a quick cutting off of the voice, and then a soft thud.

More intrigued than ever, Tinker waited to see what would follow. Not a sound came. He chafed as the minutes passed, for he knew Soto must be indulging in something of prime importance to— Soto. At last Blake's assistant could control himself no longer, so very gently he began to press with the tips of his fingers against the door.

It moved away from him with a continuous pressure against him. The spring was strong enough once the door was away from the vertical hand, and in a way Tinker welcomed this, for the slightest release of his fingers would allow it to swing back into place.

Bit by bit he thrust it away from him until the tiny crack widened to the space of an inch or so. And then, all at once, he caught sight of the Jap in such a position that Tinker's eyes widened in amazement.

He was on his knees before a small shining electric cooking-stove. On top of the stove was a small idol of the Buddha, and, on either side of the statue, a long thin vase in which burned sticks of incense. They had just been lighted, the pungent odour only now reaching Tinker's nostrils. The Jap's attitude was one of profound absorption, but as his back was towards the watcher, Tinker could not see whether his eyes were open or closed.

Then all of a sudden Tinker's gaze was caught by something else. Just back of Soto on the floor was a small japanned box about two feet long by eighteen inches wide and a foot or so high. Close beside it lay a green canvas bag, and now, as his eyes again went back to the Jap, Tinker saw that he was in the act of making obeisance to the Buddha with the palm of each hand facing the floor. It was the sign in the East given by one when asking a blessing of the Buddha before undertaking a long journey! Soto was going away!

Where? And how?

The two questions flashed into Tinker's mind as realisation came to him. There could be no doubt about it. As the figment of some long-hazy dream he remembered that once, when Blake had taken him to see some Japanese actors in Nagasaki, the plot of the thing had been a most complicated arrangement of certain phases of village life.

Tinker never could have given a sketch of the whole play, for the reason that it lasted for nearly nine hours, and he was dozing for part of the time. But in one scene the hero, or the villain —he could not recall which—had been about to embark upon a journey, and he had sung a monotonous little song just as Soto had sung, after which he had prostrated himself in devotion before the Buddha in just this way. The Jap was about to fly—where?

Tinker would have given a good deal just then if Blake had been with him. But the detective was not there, so he must act on his own initiative. Blake had said, in Farquhar's bungalow, that he considered Soto an important factor in the case. Therefore Blake would want the Jap placed somewhere within his knowledge so that he could deal with him if need be.

Blake had said also that if Soto could be made to talk he could give the full yarn of what had happened at the bungalow on the night of the murder. Therefore Soto must not be allowed to fade away; and, hard on that, Tinker remembered the yacht of mystery which was again lying just offshore.

It was enough. The Jap must be stopped. And now was the time to stop him.

Still pressing gently he got the door open to the extent of another eighteen inches. Then he thrust one rubber-clad sole over the threshold. His shoulder held the door in position while his body advanced. Then the other foot followed, and still a third step put him fully into the room. With fingers gripping the edge of the door he was just easing it back into place when suddenly the spring gave a little squeak.

The sound reached the kneeling Jap, who sat for a moment as if he did not dream that anyone else could be in the room. Then ever so slowly his head turned and turned and turned until Tinker, fascinated by the extraordinary amount of pivot control in the neck, thought it must snap. But his thoughts came back with a jerk to the job in hand as a pair of expressionless brown eyes rested on his.

Not the faintest flicker of surprise did the Jap show—just looked and looked as if he had a quite detached interest in the intruder. But well it was for Tinker that he knew the race, for with lightning-like rapidity, as if he had been propelled upwards by steel springs—the Jap was on his feet, a long-bladed Malay kris in his hand, and murder in his intent as he sprang at Tinker.

14.   A Fight for Life.

IT would have been possible for Tinker to use his automatic. He was as quick on the "draw" as any of the spectacular gentlemen presented for our amusement and edification on the films. Coached by Blake, he had, even as a youth, developed an uncanny aptitude in the handling of firearms, and it would have been simple enough for him to have whipped out the weapon from the side-pocket of his coat while the Jap was still a yard away.

In Tinker's mind, however, was the thought that the yacht lay moored so close. A shot, even within the walls of the back room of the bungalow, would carry a long way on such a still night, and particularly so over water.

The clearness with which Tinker had heard the strumming on board was sufficient proof of that. And something told him that whatever passed between him and the Jap must be finished without the knowledge of those on board the yacht.

So, instead of clawing for his automatic, he threw himself to one side, just as Soto brought the kris round and up in a slashing blow that would have opened Tinker wide had that point ever reached his body. It was the orthodox knife attack of the Japanese, just as the disembowelling slash is the stroke of the Gurkha with the deadly, curved kukri. And the most effective counter to it was one which would not have been used in Western methods of fighting. In a case, however, where it was his life against the other, Tinker had no qualms about using it. To meet Oriental attack one must use Oriental defence.

So, while Soto tried desperately to recover his balance, Tinker came into action. Like a flash his right knee came up waist high, and then all the force of his body and thigh was concentrated in the thrust as he drove his foot into the Jap's stomach.

A man of twenty stone could not have stood up against that terrific drive; and the Jap did not weigh more than seven or eight. A deep grunt of agony escaped him as he doubled up and went flying back, to fetch up with a bang against the wall that knocked him nearly senseless. The knife clattered to the floor, and, before he could succeed in his desperate effort to retrieve it, Tinker was upon him.

Blake's protege did not make the mistake of thinking Soto had shot his bolt when he lost the knife, or that he had no more tricks in his bag. If he could weather the storm until the breath once more filled his tortured lungs and depressed his outraged diaphragm, he would still be as dangerous as active dynamite, for no Jap who wandered the world, as had this specimen—who had adopted a crooked way of life on two sides of the globe—would be unequipped with the national physical art of his country —ju-jutsu.

Tinker had passed in that form of offence and defence just as he had had to acquire a working knowledge of all other recognised forms of physical combat. It had been a necessary part of his training, and he was no slouch at the game; but he knew that he would stand little chance against a Jap, who was finished in the art once the other got a master hold. So he set himself to finish off the other before his desperate lungs should fill again.

Again and again he tried to land his fist on Soto's jaw. Despite the agony within him, and the necessity to yield his body to the pain, the Jap used a rapid, swaying motion that beat Tinker time after time. His knuckles would slide past by the barest fraction of an inch from the vital point; the Jap seemed to know that, at all costs, he must dodge the full force of those blows until he could come into action.

And, at last, in a wild determination to send his man down for keeps, Tinker came thrashing in, swinging a pair of haymakers that carried a terrific kick in each.

The Jap met the attack by slumping suddenly to the floor. Tinker's knuckles encountered nothing but the wall, and, with an imprecation, he flung himself back as the Jap grabbed him by the knees. It brought Tinker down with a crash, and then every orthodox form of fighting went by the board as the pair fought and scrambled like a pair of wild cats to reach the knife.

Tinker's longer arms gave him the advantage at the critical moment. He could not reach far enough to get his fingers round the handle, but he managed to push the knife farther away, and then he found his whole attention concentrated on his antagonist, for, seeing that the knife was now out of his calculations, Soto had twisted round like an eel, bringing up one arm in the deadly ju-jutsu neckhold which dragged Tinker's head down until his spine threatened to crack.

The first agony of the hold drew a gasp of pain. But as the Jap, with a sound of breath whistling through his teeth, exerted himself to the full to snap the spinal cord, Tinker made a desperate twist to get his elbow in, in the only counter that would serve. He thought every bone would be torn loose in the spinal column as he did so. The sweat came out on his forehead in great beads of acute agony. But he persisted, and then, as he jammed his elbow in with a sharp drive, he felt the least bit of lessening in the deadly hold.

Again he jammed his elbow in and up under his arm, watching his chance. The Jap was forced to allow his arm to slip the merest trifle. It was that for which Tinker was watching. Like lightning his own hand went up under, and a surprised exclamation came in a jerk from the other's lips as he realised his opponent was using the major counter in ju-jutsu—one that only a student of all five classes could have acquired.

"A-i-a!"

The squeal was one of terrible agony as Tinker's fingers closed round the Jap's wrist and dragged his arm round. Next, despite the frantic efforts of the other to bring in the eleventh counter. Tinker got it up and back over his shoulder; then, slowly, but determinedly, he got to his feet.

He bent, he straightened suddenly, and then the Jap went flying clean over his shoulder, to land with a terrific crash against the electric stove. Down tumbled the statue of the Buddha, and into the broken bits of baked earth rolled Soto, one arm twisted under him in a way that told its own tale.

But Tinker knew the job was not yet finished. The Jap would pull all the tricks he knew in order to get away now, for he must realise that Tinker could be no stray canvasser such as he appeared. The Jap's quick wits would sense that the intrusion had some connection with the murder, and, if he had a story to suppress, then his hope of doing so lay in the next few minutes.

Another mind was working just as fast as the Jap's. That brain was Tinker's, and it was a fleeting glimpse of the japanned box and green canvas bag that caused him to remember that Soto had been on the point of leaving. If there were some chance that he had been going aboard the yacht, why was it lying off the bungalow? And he certainly couldn't swim if he were going that way! Which meant if he were going that way a boat might be coming ashore for him.

Tinker didn't have time then to figure the whys or the wherefores of the problem. He had only time to jump the Jap before the latter began slithering like an eel towards the door which gave on to the back veranda.

Despite his broken arm, Soto fought like a cornered rat, but when it became plain that this white youth must master him, he opened his mouth wide. A high-pitched yell was just beginning in his throat when Tinker's fingers closed over his windpipe. Then there followed a short, sharp tussle, at the end of which the Jap went suddenly limp in Tinker's' grasp. Watchful for tricks, the young detective eased his hold, and then, picking up the Jap as if he had been a bundle of old rags, he slung him over his shoulder, taking care that his head hung forwards so that his fingers could reach his windpipe quickly in case he tried again to yell.

Holding him thus, Tinker cast about him for signs of cord. From one wall to a corner ran a length of thin clothes line on which a few cloths had been hung to dry. Tinker dragged this down with one jerk, and, stuffing it into his pocket, staggered through the door with his burden.

He made straight for the cover of the trees, his object being to bind and gag Soto in some safe place while he investigated further into the bungalow, and, if it were possible, make a closer surveillance of the yacht. Then he would take his prisoner back to Hollywood with him. He didn't know what else to do with him. It hadn't been on the cards that he was to capture the Jap and abduct him; but, then, he didn't know he was to find him on the point of clearing when he got there. And Blake had told him to use his own judgment when he saw how things were going.

Tinker couldn't tell what Blake would think of this unexpected guest, but he was still convinced that Soto must not be left to his own devices after what had happened.

There were complications ahead, Tinker could see. For Instance, the Jap had been left as caretaker by the police. Supposing they should wish to interview him and should find him gone? Well, Tinker reflected, if he was any judge of the signs, Soto would have been gone anyway.

Again, if he had been trying to reach the yacht, then the chances were a boat would come ashore for him. Supposing it might be on its way even now—what would those who came in it think when they found no signs of the Jap?

It was that thought that caused Tinker to dump his burden into some bushes closer to the bungalow than he had intended. Then he made quick work of the tying and gagging of him, making sure that the knots were such that not even a slippery Oriental could worm his way out of them.

He had been thinking for some time that Soto had been remarkably quiet, and now he risked flashing his pocket torch upon him as he surveyed the completed job. He understood when he saw the chalk tinge on the Jap's face and his closed eyes; he had fainted.

Leaving him there, Tinker switched off the torch and started back stealthily for the bungalow. His immediate purpose was to get hold of Soto's japanned box and canvas bag. It occurred to him that there might be some quite interesting items to be found in them. But before he had covered half the distance a sound reached him, causing him to sink down quickly into the cover of a small clump of trees.

No sooner had he had done so than he heard the sound still nearer. He strained his ears to listen, and then he knew that someone was running lightly down one of the footpaths towards the bungalow, panting as they came.

15. The Secret of Sonia Vensky.

TINKER landed in the path with a soft thud, and started after those pattering footsteps. So faint were they now that it was difficult for him to tell exactly which way they had gone, proving that the person who had passed was moving cautiously despite his haste. But the general direction had been towards the bungalow, so Tinker made that way.

As he neared it, however, he came into a walk, and then as the faint outline of the low, squat building loomed just ahead of him, he dropped to his hands and knees. Crouching thus, he listened. He could see no sign of the person who had come that way, nor could he hear sound of movement within the bungalow. But somehow he felt that his quarry must have had the building as objective.

Who could it be? Was it some person who had come in haste to see the Jap? Could it be someone connected with Sonia Vensky? Or might it be a messenger from Plummer and Vali Mata-Vali? At any rate, that person had come in great haste, and Tinker made up his mind he would see if he had entered the bungalow.

Crawling cautiously, he skirted the front and reached the other side on which the dining-room window looked. Darkness as before, except for the glow of light that came from behind the red curtain in the kitchen. Then, suddenly, Tinker saw a shadow pass across the window. Someone was in the kitchen.

He got cautiously to his feet and covered the few feet which separated him from the side veranda. A single stretch of the foot landed him on it, and, like a shadow, he passed into the dark dining-room. Keeping well clear of the table, he crossed into the hall. He knew the way now, so a few cautious strides carried him round the bend of the hall and along until he was opposite the swing door which connected with the kitchen.

There he paused, and now he could distinctly hear the sounds of someone moving in the room. He stole forward, intending to spy in the same way as he had spied upon Soto, and his fingers were just in the act of pushing the door open a trifle when, without warning, he was jerked inwards, and he found himself gazing into the black mouth of a heavy automatic pistol. Then he straightened up, gasping to keep from exploding, for it was Sexton Blake!

"Where the deuce have you been?" asked Blake, in a savage

whisper. "This room looks as if the house was being broken up. Where is the Jap? I came here at top speed to get hold of you; there isn't a moment to lose."

"I found the Jap in here. He was on the point of clearing out. We had a set-to, and I got the better of him— broke his arm. He is bound and gagged out in the garden. He is quite safe. I think he had some idea of getting away on the yacht."

Blake's frown passed.

"Good! I feared something had gone wrong. Keep the Jap where he is. You had better get into the garden and lie low there. Sonia Vensky will be here any minute. Don't show yourself unless you hear a signal from me. Now clear, and as you go through turn on one light—the one over the table in the dining-room."

Tinker turned and sped back the way he had come. Blake paused only long enough to take another look round the kitchen, then he followed the way his assistant had gone. But when he entered the dining-room he did not pass through to the veranda.

Instead, he secreted himself behind the curtains at the side of the french windows, and after one glance at the shaded light over the table, arranged them so they completely hid him from view. They were the same curtains from behind which Blake had suggested that the shot which had killed Posani might have been fired. Then, silence in the bungalow.

Five minutes, ten minutes passed, and now came the faint throb of an engine from somewhere near the road. It grew more and more audible until it was quite near the bungalow; then it suddenly stopped. Followed another period of silence, and then the faint crunch of a step on the gravel of the path. A footfall on the veranda, and slow, halting steps as someone came round the veranda, as if looking for a means of entering.

Then the steps retreated, and a few moments later a bell shrilled somewhere within the bungalow. There was another silence, after which the bell rang again; no response.

A third ring was equally barren of result, and again the footsteps came round the veranda. This time they continued on until they reached the open french windows of the dining-room. Another pause, followed by a tentative footfall, as the person stepped into the room.

The feet moved across until the owner of them stood by the table, which was still laid as for the demonstration which had taken place earlier in the day. And now a woman's voice rose, hesitant, cautious, trembling.

"Soto!"

No answer, and the footsteps continued to the curtains which screened the room from the hall.

"Soto!"

The call went echoing down the passage. But there came no answer.

Again the footsteps could be heard moving towards the kitchen, and, growing fainter and fainter, they finally died away. Another silence before the sound, more hesitant now than ever, came again.

Slowly the person returned and entered the dining-room. Haltingly the feet moved towards the table, and there came a deep sigh, followed by the scraping of a chair as someone sat down.

A slight tinkle of silver could be heard, as if something on the table were being pushed away, then another silence, broken only by the ticking of the long grandfather clock which stood against one wall.

Came the slightest possible movement of the curtains by the french window. Then, ever so slowly, an arm appeared, the hand grasping a heavy automatic pistol, which rose until it was pointing straight over the shoulder of the person who sat in the chair which Peter J. Constant had occupied on the night of the tragedy.

A moment thus, then the curtains moved again, a little higher up, and now a head appeared, the upper part of the features being concealed by a black silk mask. Through the narrow slits a pair of eyes watched the woman who sat at the table.

She was dressed in a long fawn silk motoring coat and small cloche hat. Her tan gloves had been tossed on the table, and her head was supported by both hands, which were cupped under her chin.

She seemed to be staring across at the seat which the Italian had occupied when he had been killed, and now another deep sigh came from her, indicating—what?

From between the lips of the masked man who watched her there broke a soft, sibilant hiss. The woman in the armchair stiffened as if a snake was close to her; but she did not turn at once. Instead, she just sat there motionless, but, had one been opposite her, one would have seen that her eyes had gone wide with nameless terror.

Again came that low hissing sound, and then, slowly, oh, so

slowly, the woman's head began to turn. Round it came, little by little, until her fearful gaze was almost at right angles to the table. She moved her body in unison now, and her eyes travelled on until suddenly she saw the steady hand which gripped the automatic.

Like one struck dumb in some terrible fascination, her gaze followed along the arm and up, up, up until she was looking at the masked countenance. She was riveted by the sardonic smile which was now showing on the thin lips, and by the hint of mockery which came from the slits of the mask.

She half rose, and her mouth opened as if she would scream; but with a terrific effort she controlled herself, biting her knuckles hard in the effort. She sank back into her chair, and as her hand lowered to grip the arm a whisper was torn from her dry lips.

"Who—who are you?"

"I am the One Who Knows," came the answer in low, deep tones.

Her eyes became more terrified than ever, if that were possible.

"What—do—you—mean?" she gasped at last.

A tall figure stepped from behind the curtain, standing in full view. The eyes seemed to burn upon her through those slits in the black silk, and now the arm that held the pistol was lowered.

"I am the One Who Knows," came the dread words again. "I have been waiting for you, Sonia Vensky, for I KNEW YOU WOULD COME."

As he finished speaking he walked forward slowly, passing close to her as she watched him in fascinated terror and going round until he stood beside the other chair. Then he sat down and faced her.

"You came to find Soto," he went on in the same inexorable tone. "But you came too late. Soto is no longer here to serve you, and it is as well for you, because Soto betrayed you."

"Ah!"

How deeply the shaft had struck home was indicated by the complete terror of that exclamation.

"For the love of heaven, tell me who you are," whispered she.

"I have already answered—I am the One Who Knows—who knows the truth of the murder of Paolo Posani!"

"I—I know nothing of it," she whispered, her eyes casting about desperately as if she would take flight.

"You do not speak the truth," came the cold tones accusingly. "It will not do to lie to me. I know what evil greed influenced you, Sonia

Vensky. I am the One Who Knows, and I shall give the truth to the world. If you would save yourself you have little time to speak. I know how you plotted against the man who lies charged of the murder; I know how you would have played one against the other so that you could get possession of great wealth. I know that things did not go as you planned, and I know whither the money has gone. You did not get it, Sonia Vensky, you got nothing. And Paolo Posani is dead. Peter J. Constant sat where you sit now, but Peter Constant did not kill Posani. I am the One Who Knows."

She passed her tongue over ashen lips. Her eyes were probing into those narrow slits, trying, trying desperately to read the identity of the man behind the mask. But the sardonic lips and the deep voice baffled her; they were not those of any person she could place. Then who was this mysterious person who knew the truth?

She was getting her nerves under control, and her agile mind was working fast. At first she had been so shocked with terror at the sight of the pistol and the masked countenance appearing in that room, where murder had been done only a few hours before —so puzzled over the unaccountable absence of the Jap, that she had snapped for a moment. But now she was herself again, and her voice was more steady as she spoke.

"You choose to speak in riddles," she said, with a hint of contempt in her voice. "I do not know you, nor why you should secrete yourself here to try to frighten me, when I come to spend a few quiet moments where the tragedy occurred of which my husband has been accused. I am here to find, if possible, something that will help him."

The lips under the mask curled.

"Your intelligence doesn't work on a very high scale if you think to gull me with that sort of talk," came the response. "You came here to find the Jap. I have already told you that he has betrayed you. You gave yourself away when you first found you were not alone. You will find that I speak the truth when I say I am the One Who Knows. You are very close to disaster, Sonia Vensky. And in this affair Fate will not be so kind as on one occasion in—Warsaw."

The blood ebbed from the woman's face and throat so swiftly as to leave them startlingly white. Her eyes became pools of complete terror and her mouth dropped loosely as that last word came out. This masked man could be nothing less than the devil. Who in all

California knew anything about—Warsaw?

That business had taken place years before—there had been only a few vague whispers against her, and she had had nothing directly to do with the killing of the violinist who had been found floating in the river.

It was true that he had been madly in love with her and had given her all he had; it was true, too, that a wild young count from Courland had fallen desperately in love with her, had lavished money and gifts on her, and this had caused acute jealousy on the part of the violinist.

There had been trouble—she had told the count that she would go away with him, only she was frightened of the violinist. Then the musician had been found in the river, and she had been free of him. But she had nothing to do with it—oh, no, not she! She could not help it if evil tongues said she had inspired the young count to kill the other.

But this person who sat opposite her could not be referring to that. It was impossible that anyone could know. It was done with and forgotten long, long ago. He was some charlatan who was only trying to frighten her. But he would find he had met his match.

She raised her eyes and stared defiantly into those two oval slits. But the sinister figure shook his head.

"It won't do, Sonia Vensky; I know what is passing in your mind. It is not forgotten that Serge Voronski was found floating in the river; it is still remembered that young Count Faranov fled into Russia. Have I not told you I am the One Who Knows?"

Her hands dropped. Serge Voronski! Count Faranov! Those names! Serge Voronski, the violinist; Count Faranov, the young Courlander who had killed him. Then it had not been forgotten; this man did not lie when he said he KNEW. But how—how—how? That old affair in Warsaw brought up here in this bungalow in California.

Suddenly a deep fear, different from the other, gripped the woman at the heart. This man meant what he said. The shadow of St. Quentin, that great stone prison, loomed above her. She saw herself caught up in the toils of the web which she herself had helped to spin. Paolo Posani was not to be allowed to remain dead, and Peter Constant was not to go to the electric chair for his murder as she had believed.

Suddenly the masked man leaned forward until his eyes bored into hers. She could see now that they were grey —a hard granite grey that was merciless.

"Do you believe now that I am the One Who Knows?" he asked harshly.

She nodded mutely. Her dry lips could not form the word.

"Then hark ye, Sonia Vensky. Your only hope is to speak this night, nor to leave unanswered one question which I shall ask. Lies will not avail you; there will be no repetition of the affair of Serge Voronski and Count Paranov. Paolo Posani was murdered, but Peter Constant did not kill him. The shot which killed him was fired from behind those curtains where I stood to-night, and you were close to this room at the time! I give you this chance to speak. Are you going to take it?"

She struggled hard in one last desperate effort to convince herself that she need have nothing to fear. But that cold, threatening gaze beat upon her in wave upon wave, and at last a faint whisper broke from her lips.

"What do you want to know?"

"The truth."

It was nearly an hour later when Sonia Vensky stumbled forth from that bungalow and started back to where she had parked her two-seater. Beside her walked a tall, masked figure; and, stealing after them, came another shadowy figure. The masked man helped her into the car, and then, just before she started off, he bent forward, murmuring a low warning.

"Remember!"

"I shall keep my instructions," she stammered; and then he allowed her to go.

He stood watching until the red rear light winked out of sight, and for a few minutes after that, until the throb of the engine had completely died away. He seemed to know that the shadowy form of the one who had followed them was close at hand, for, turning his head just a little, he whispered:

"Come here, Tinker; there is the question of the yacht still to deal with."

16.   The Japanese Prisoner.

SCARCELY had Blake whispered his warning to his assistant than there reached them the muffled sound of what could only be oars moving in rowlocks. Blake caught Tinker's arm, and started in a noiseless trot back towards the bungalow. They dodged into cover near the veranda, and then Tinker followed Blake, as the detective crawled along through the bushes to a point where he could overlook the little jetty.

It was much darker now, for clouds had come over during the past half-hour, but he could still make out the patch that marked the jetty, and now they could plainly hear someone rowing ashore from, they presumed, the yacht.

Shortly after that the sound of the oars ceased, and, a little later, the soft patter of footsteps sounded as someone walked quickly up the jetty. Blake put out a tentative hand, finding he could actually touch the gravel of the path. Flattening himself back suddenly, he was just in time to avoid a boot-heel on his head as a man crunched past.

He made straight for the bungalow, and then they could hear him stumbling along by the side. Blake twisted his head towards Tinker, who was lying flat beside him.

"You were right," he breathed. "There is only one, though; he has come ashore for the Jap. There may be another in the boat."

At this moment the sound of a low whistle reached them, then a short silence followed by another whistle. A third and a fourth time the sound was repeated, after which they could hear, faintly, movements as if the man had entered the bungalow.

Following that he returned and started down the path towards the jetty. It was just as he came abreast of where Blake and Tinker lay— which was on the edge of the slope at the point where the bushes ended and the approach to the little jetty began— that he drew up and gave another whistle.

This time his signal was answered from the end of the jetty, proving the correctness of Blake's surmise that another man had been left with the boat. A voice, low, but startlingly clear on the still night air, reached them. And it told Blake all he needed to know, when he grasped that the man was using the Moorish tongue of northern Africa.

"Why do you whistle?" was what he said.

"There is no one to be seen outside or in," was the guarded answer in the same language.

"The little yellow infidel—is he not there?"

"Nay."

"But he was to be waiting; it was orders, and understood."

"He has been there. I have seen a quantity of 'saman' (luggage). There is also one of his accursed gods lying broken on the floor. But of him there is no sign."

"He must be about. Take another look, if you want me I shall help you."

"If I whistle, come."

With that, the man in the path turned and stumped back towards the bungalow. They could hear him plainly this time, using less caution as he searched high and low for the Jap. It was while this was going on that Blake laid a cautious finger on Tinker's arm.

"Wait here," he whispered. "If the man in the boat comes up before I return, club him with your pistol as he passes. If not, leave it to me."

With that, Blake was away like a shadow. He used cover in getting close to the bungalow, but once he was at one side he made no attempt to disguise his approach. A sudden cessation of sound within told him he had been heard, so dodging to one side of the back door he jerked out his pistol and waited, the weapon being reversed in his hand.

Only a few moments passed, and then the door opened to permit a hulking, oddly clad fellow to emerge. Blake spotted him at once as typical of the seafaring men one may find in any seaport along the north coast of Africa, and then, as the fellow stepped completely out, he struck just once. The Moor went down like a log in the path.

Blake slipped into the kitchen, and followed Tinker's example by purloining some clothes-line. With this he bound the Moor securely, gagging him with a bit of his own short jacket. Then he sped back to the path, pausing at the crest of the dip to give a warning whisper to Tinker before emitting a whistle as he had heard the other signal.

The answer came promptly. As a matter of fact, by now, the man who waited with the boat was getting anxious about the long absence of his companion, and, as soon as he gave the response, Blake could hear him say in Moorish;

"Why do you not come?"

"Come and see," was Blake's reply, muffled, so that the difference in voices would not be too apparent.

There was a slight pause, then they could hear the man's footsteps on the jetty as he approached. Blake did not move, but waited until the other was almost abreast of him. He knew that in a moment or so the fellow would note the deception, even in the gloom; but he did not wait for that. Swiftly and surely he struck with the butt of his weapon, and, with only a short grunt, the man doubled up in a heap on the ground.

"Lend a hand here, Tinker," said Blake, in a low tone. "We've got to make haste. They may be sending a hail from the yacht soon."

Together they carried their unconscious victim along to the back of the bungalow, where they bound and gagged him like his fellow. Then Blake thought for a few moments.

"We can't take the whole caboodle into Hollywood in these two small cars," he remarked. "I think we shall have to stuff them away out here some place. That lane where the cars are standing will do."

"What about the Jap, guv'nor?"

"We'll take him in with us. I want that slippery fellow where we can keep an eye on him."

"And his luggage?"

"We'll take it also."

It was the better part of twenty minutes before they had carried the two Tangerines to the spot of which Blake had spoken. There they dumped them in the cover of some thick bushes which grew at the base of a clump of cottonwoods, and, returning to where Tinker had "parked" the Jap, he heaved him on his shoulder and started back.

"You go on, Tinker; I'll bring his luggage," were Blake's words.

But Blake waited to do something else before retrieving the lacquered box and green canvas bag. Stealing down on to the jetty, he gazed out at the yacht. He would have given a good deal just then to know what the captain's orders were, and if it had returned to this anchorage just for the purpose of picking up the Jap.

He could not believe that Plummer and Vali Mata-Vali would go to all that trouble unless they were ready to make a quick getaway, and, the way Blake now had the affair in his mind, he could not see what should hold them in either Hollywood or Los Angeles, if they could elude the police.

And, while there was supposed to be a watch being kept over

them, Blake knew that while the police believed Peter J. Constant to be guilty of the murder, that surveillance would be of the most desultory kind.

As far as Blake had been able to discover, the pair had still been at their bungalow in Hollywood that afternoon; and he had very particular reasons for getting back before they could make a dash. He knew now how Paola Posani had been murdered; he could almost prove whose hand had pulled the trigger of the weapon that had been discharged from behind the curtains; and he believed that the loot which had been taken from the safe at the bungalow was in the hands of Plummer and Vali Mata-Vali.

If he could only impress the police sufficiently in order to get them into action in time! His only hope was Morrison and—the Mexican border was perilously close.

While Blake stood, there came a hail from the yacht asking what was causing the delay. He put his hands funnel-shaped over his mouth and called back a reassurance; then, bending down, he untied the boat that swung at the end of the jetty. Giving it a push, he allowed it to swing out, hoping it would drift some distance down the coast before grounding.

Then, speeding back to the bungalow, he heaved up Soto's luggage, and hastened on to where Tinker was waiting. He did not attempt to turn out the lights, but left them just as they were, with the french window of the dining-room open.

Ten minutes later, with the bound and gagged form of the Jap in his car, and the luggage in Tinker's, the two started back at top speed for Hollywood.

17. The Drug Test.

WHEN Sexton Blake entered the large, well-furnished library of Farquhar's bungalow on his return to Hollywood, he was amazed to see Peter J. Constant seated opposite the attorney. Farquhar gave Blake a sidelong look as the detective shook hands with the millionaire.

"Where have you been?" he asked. "I thought you had kept on going right out of the State."

"I'll tell you in a moment. But how does Mr. Constant come here? I take it you were successful in arranging bail."

Farquhar grinned.

"I told you I would pull some strings. But didn't you spot the two plainclothes men, front and back, as you came in?"

Blake turned quickly.

"No; I hope to goodness they didn't spot us. Tinker and I have been doing some kidnapping. We had better leave everything else until we put the 'signs of our crime' out of sight."

"What do you mean?"

Blake explained in a few cogent words how Tinker, had overpowered the Jap, and how he had thought it wiser to bring him along to Hollywood.

"He is a witness we must have," he went on. "I shall tell you the whole yarn presently, but first we must get him out of sight. Have you a spare room here where we can lock him up? And he will have to have the attention of a doctor—Tinker was compelled to break his arm—the little yellow fiend tried to strangle him."

"Plenty of rooms here, Blake. I'll ring, and we shall fix him up at once. And we couldn't do better than get Dr. Thornton—he is the specialist who made the pathological examination of Mr. Constant."

Blake shot a quick look of inquiry from one to the other, and the attorney nodded.

"These police fellows in Hollywood are due for a shock when they read the result of that, Blake. It is one of the most marvellous bits of detective stuff I have ever come across. I've read of that sort of thing, but I never expected to see it in real life."

Blake flushed; he hated praise.

"I take it, then, that something was found?"

"You just wait. Let us fix up that Jap first, and 'phone for Dr.

Thornton. I've got some things to tell you that will interest you."

Peter J. Constant, a very chastened man, waited in the library until they returned. It would appear that they must have come into the garage without the Jap being spotted by the plainclothes men who were outside to shadow Constant should he move abroad, for they saw no signs of them.

They locked the Jap in an upstairs room, and, when a message had been put through to Dr. Thornton, they returned to the library.

"Now I'll tell you," said Farquhar, as he pushed the cigars across. "Thornton made a pathological examination of Mr. Constant's blood, stomach, and tissues. You were absolutely right, Blake. He found in the stomach traces of a most potent drug which took him a long time to identify. In fact, it wasn't until he had made a blood test that he succeeded in doing so. What he came across was only the remnants of what must have been in Mr. Constant's system; but it was enough, and he can prove beyond the shadow of a doubt that Mr. Constant was drugged by 'seroin' within the last forty-eight hours. And, of all mediums by which it could be surreptitiously introduced into the system, none would be a better medium than brandy."

Blake nodded thoughtfully.

"Seroin—eh? That clinches what I wanted, Farquhar. The effect would be just what Mr. Constant experienced."

Here the millionaire looked up quickly.

"I am entirely in the hands of you and Mr. Farquhar, Mr. Blake," he said hoarsely, "and I am not going to ask any worrying questions, but can you give me any hope?"

Blake looked at him with a friendly smile.

"You can cast aside all anxiety, Mr. Constant. There are one or two other items I wish to clear up, but before another twenty-four hours are passed the world will know that you did not kill Paolo Posani."

The millionaire half-started up in the intense wave of relief that overwhelmed him.

"You—you know who did it, Mr. Blake?" he gasped.

"I know how it was done, and I know that you did not do it, Mr. Constant. I hope, before I have finished, to put my hands on the murderer. And now, Farquhar, what else?"

"The note which Mr. Constant received, or believed to have come from Posani. I have made an exhaustive comparison of that with other writings of his, and have had Connel, the handwriting expert, on it as well. We can prove beyond the shadow of a doubt that it is a forgery."

"Good! That is one most important link."

"And I hope to have another this evening. It is with regard to the note which Posani said he received from Mr. Constant. We couldn't find it among the papers which we got hold of, but I have one of my best men at his private studio, and we have used a little bribery with one of the men who worked with Posani. I am hoping—Yes?"

This as a knock came at the door. The interruption was caused by Dr. Thornton, the specialist, who was introduced to Blake and Tinker, and they went off at once to look after the Jap. He promised to give Blake a copy of the results of the pathological examination he had made, and they were just settling down again when a further interruption came.

This was Farquhar's man who had been poking about in search of the note to which the attorney had referred, and when Farquhar returned to the library it was triumphantly to wave the piece of paper. He showed it at once to the millionaire, who, after a careful perusal of the writing, shook his head vigorously.

"It is a forgery," he said emphatically. "I never wrote that; any independent test will show that it couldn't be mine, although it is a mighty good imitation."

"Good!" exclaimed Blake. "We shall have that tested by your handwriting expert the first thing in the morning, Farquhar. In the meantime, will you take care of it? We shall use it as Exhibit 'C' or 'D' unless I am mistaken."

When Farquhar had placed the document in the safe he looked towards Blake.

"And now what about it?" he asked.

"I should prefer to get through as soon as possible to Detective Morrison," was Blake's answer. "I have got here just what I needed; and now I can give Morrison the names of the person who should be arrested and charged with the murder of Paolo Posani. But, unless I am mistaken, it will be necessary to act immediately. I greatly fear that the persons in question will try to make a getaway to-night."

"You would rather keep the whole story until then?"

"Yes, but I shall tell you the names now if you wish."

"We should be most interested."

Blake glanced towards Peter J. Constant. He knew the actual

accusation would be a good deal of a shock to him, but after what he had already passed through, Blake did not think the millionaire could have retained much nonsense in him for the beautiful Vali Mata-Vali, who had succeeded in making such a fool of him. So, without further hesitation, he shot out the names.

"Madame Vali Mata-Vali and her 'director,' Senor Machado."

The millionaire gave a startled gasp.

"She—she could not have shot Posani in cold blood! And what could her motive be?"

Blake smiled faintly.

"She did not pull the trigger, Mr. Constant. But she planned a good deal of it. It was Machado who did the actual killing. And I am afraid you must prepare yourself for a further shock. Your wife—Sonia Vensky—was also implicated in the affair, but not in conjunction with Vali Mata-Vali and Machado. She did not plan Posani's death, but had you been killed it would not have been the other two we should seek this night."

Constant went grey.

"You—mean—" he stammered.

"I mean it was a fortunate thing for you that a more subtle plan was afoot with Posani as the intended victim. You will understand later. You would have been the catspaw in any case, for it was you who had the millions that certain unscrupulous people sought; but, in the other case, you would have been a dead catspaw, and—Posani would have been your murderer. But I think we had better try to get through to Morrison. Will you see if you can get in touch, Farquhar?"

Highly intrigued over Blake's definite statements, the attorney lost no time in putting through a call. Morrison was not at police headquarters, nor could three other calls find him. It was Blake who at last suggested that they might reach him at Constant's private suite in the Imperial Hotel, so a call was put through to Los Angeles. And it was there that they found him.

On hearing that Sexton Blake had a most important communication to make, he agreed to motor out to Hollywood at once. While they were waiting Dr. Thornton appeared to announce that he had done what he could for the Jap, and that now he was fairly comfortable, with Farquhar's manservant sitting on guard over him. Then the doctor glanced towards Tinker.

"It strikes me, from what I have seen, that you bested him rather badly at his own game, young man."

"Is it a bad smash?" asked Tinker, flushing.

The specialist smiled.

"You have made a mess of his elbow, and there is a compound fracture of the upper arm—if you call that 'bad.' And now, Mr. Blake, I shall be pleased to give you the result of my pathological examination of Mr. Constant," added the specialist, turning to the detective. But Blake explained that they were waiting for Detective Morrison, and asked if he could arrange to wait so that Morrison could hear what he had to say. The specialist agreed to this, so they sat talking of the case in general, finding their comments naturally a little reserved in front of Constant, until Morrison arrived. He bustled in with a handshake for everyone, then in bluff tones he rallied Blake.

"Well, what is this important matter you wish to communicate. Mr. Blake?"

"We wish to request you to make a double arrest to-night in connection with the murder of Paolo Posani," answered Blake coolly. "I am not a citizen of the State of California, but Mr. Farquhar is, and can swear out the necessary charge."

"A double arrest? B-but what on earth do you mean? Who are the people?"

"A woman known as Madame Vali Mata-Vali and her business director, one Senor Machado. The latter is the one who actually killed Posani."

The American slumped into a chair and smiled in amused fashion.

"With all due respect to Mr. Constant, who is here, I cannot take that seriously, Mr. Blake. How on earth do you get that idea in your head?"

Blake did not lose his temper. He had expected incredulity on the part of Morrison, but he knew that he had that within his arsenal by which he should confound him before he finished. So his voice was perfectly quiet as he said:

"Mr. Morrison, you have been in the game of criminal detection for a good many years. Like myself, there are certain international criminals whose names ring more familiar than others; there are, I am sure, wrongdoers who are still at large and at work whose crimes bear certain earmarks by which you feel you know the hand that did the deed."

The other nodded.

"Sure, Mr. Blake. There are half a dozen or more I could name. But they will drop into the net one of these days."

"Quite so; that is my own opinion. And to-night I am hopeful that one whose name must be almost as well known to you as to me will meet his Waterloo."

"If you mean this bird Machado, I don't recognise the name."

"I have not yet seen Senor Machado, but I am going to risk what reputation I may have as a criminologist by saying that he is a man whose real name would be well known to you as a master criminal."

"The name—what is it?"

"George Marsden Plummer."

Morrison's eyes widened.

"George Marsden Plummer! Your English crook who used to be an inspector at Scotland Yard?"

"The same."

"But I heard he was dead. I haven't heard anything about him for some years."

"He was for about eight years in the Riff country of Morocco. He was known there as Sakre-el-Drooge, the Hawk of the Peak, and was captain of the front-line fighting troops of the notorious Abdel-Krim, the Lion of the Riff. When Abdel-Krim surrendered to the French last year Plummer was out of a job, so to speak. Then he reappeared on the stage of European crime in a most sensational affair in Paris, in which his partner was Madame Vali Mata-Vali. They succeeded in escaping from the French police and dropped out of sight until I heard of them here. I am almost certain that you will find the pseudo-Spaniard, Machado, is none other but Plummer."

"You certainly interest me, Mr. Blake, but will you tell me how you connect them with the killing of Posani. Why on earth should they want to bump him off? I knew—er—ahem!— excuse me, Mr. Constant, for speaking plainly—I knew that the lady was very friendly with Mr. Constant, and it is up to him to say whether the rumours that he was about to elope with her are true or not; but what had Posani to do with it? I should have thought you would have tried to find a better counter-charge than that, Mr. Blake. It is difficult for me to speak plainly in front of Mr. Constant, but you asked me to come, and if he remains I can't help it."

"I believe Mr. Constant would prefer to remain, and you need not fear that you will offend him, Mr. Morrison, because he is an innocent man, and tomorrow the world will know it. But I believe time is precious, and I ask you again if you will make the double arrest?"

"Not unless you give me better grounds than you have, Mr. Blake. I am sorry, but I stand on the police case."

"But you do not want to allow the guilty persons to escape, I take it?"

"You hang something definite on to that pair, and you'll see how fast I go after them," returned the American grimly.

Suddenly Blake came to his feet.

"Very well," he said curtly, "I shall lay all my cards on the table before these witnesses; and if you don't take action after that, then we shall make a higher appeal. But for personal reasons I wanted it to be you who made the arrest. Listen, all of you, here is the tale of what happened that night at the bungalow when Posani was killed. Have I your permission, Mr. Constant, to use names and incidents frankly?"

"Go the limit, Mr. Blake; spare no one."

18. Blake's Story.

"WE are all au fait with Mr. Constant's earlier connection with Madame Vali Mata-Vali," went on Blake, when he had lighted a cigar. "He met her in Paris and proposed marriage. His offer was refused. Then, on his return to California, he was caught on the rebound, so to speak, by a woman, who, without exception, is one of the most ruthless 'man-eaters' I have ever known. I do not think I need be guided by any consideration of the fact that she is technically Mr. Constant's wife. She was that in spirit. Her name was somewhat familiar to me, and seemed to recall vague recollections of some case which had come across my notice in the past.

"I racked my memory, and when I knew she came from Warsaw I suddenly remembered. But just to make sure I sent a cablegram to Warsaw yesterday, and this morning I had the reply. I kept this to myself until I should be able to face her with the knowledge I possessed.

"For months past this woman has been scheming how she could get hold of some of Mr. Constant's millions. Her friendship with Posani was, in my opinion, nothing more than an attempt to bring him under her complete influence, so that he would act as her tool in any plan she might evolve. She did the same thing in Warsaw, and I can give you the story if you wish.

"Well, she had fixed on no definite plan until Madame Vali Mata-Vali appeared on the scene. There was everything to make those two women hate each other. They were both actresses and both had been the object of attention from Mr. Constant. In addition, it came to Sonia Vensky's knowledge that Schwarz, of the Cosmos Film Corporation, had made an offer to Madame Vali Mata-Vali to appear in some of his productions which, in amount, broke all previous records.

Sonia Vensky was under contract to Schwarz for a small amount, and there you have the makings of a first-class conflagration without anything else.

"But there was something else. There was all the gossip that could not help reaching Sonia Vensky's ears about her husband's open infatuation for Vali Mata-Vali.

"Then, from some source which I think I can place, came an anonymous letter, which told her that Mr. Constant had realised on many millions of his investments with the object of clearing out with Vali Mata-Vali. I suspected some such letter as that, and to-night I confirmed my suspicions."

"How?" broke in Morrison quickly.

"I had it from Sonia Vensky's lips," answered Blake quietly, and before the American could speak again resumed:

"This coincided with the opening of a very effective plot which Vali Mata-Vali and her 'director' Machado had evolved for the undoing of Mr. Constant. It was easy enough for Vali Mata-Vali to produce plenty of material for the forging of his writing because she had received many letters from him written at all sorts of times, and in all sorts of moods. It was an easy enough job to get hold of some of Posani's writings, too; I think we shall eventually find that someone around his house or studio was bribed in this. At any rate, two notes were written— one purporting to be from Mr. Constant to Posani and the other from Posani to Mr. Constant. Each note made a request of the other to meet him at the bungalow in order to discuss private matters. What had they to discuss? The whole of Hollywood could answer that question, and I need not stress it. At any rate, they both kept the rendezvous.

"And here enters the play of opposing forces. Through Posani, Sonia Vensky knew of this meeting. In fact, he asked her if he should go. Her agile mind at once saw the possibilities, and she said 'yes.' From that moment she became active. Soto, the Japanese houseboy, was all that time in her confidence and pay. He was a spy on Mr. Constant's doings when he was at the bungalow alone."

Peter J. Constant was smiling crookedly now, but at a glance from Blake he nodded grimly. It was unpleasant sitting there listening to what an ass he had been, but he would grin and go through with it.

"Sonia Vensky saw that if the two men got heated through drink and argument there might well be a serious quarrel. And she primed Posani for this. She also arranged with Soto to see that the drink was served without pause, to which he agreed. And she herself was lurking about the place while the two men dined in order to see how things went. She knew the combination of the safe, and the anonymous letter she had received told her that some of the millions would be in that. But things went wrong, and instead of Posani killing Mr. Constant in a heated quarrel the Italian fell victim to a bullet which was not fired by Mr. Constant."

"Who sent the anonymous letter?" jerked Morrison.

"Vali Mata-Vali or Plummer," answered Blake promptly.

"But why should they butt in if they thought Sonia Vensky had already fixed a plot or would evolve one after getting the letter?"

"Because they did not want Constant killed. That would have been too crude. But if they could twist things by having Posani killed and make things appear that only Mr. Constant could have done it, it would involve him certainly, Sonia Vensky possibly, and leave the way clear for them to make a clean get-away with the millions."

Morrison looked impressed, but merely grunted:

"Go on, please."

"One thing that caused Sonia Vensky's plans to collapse was the transfer of service from the Japanese houseboy to Plummer. That Jap had a very bad record before he came here. Some years ago he was roustabout boy in a gin dive known as Dutch Pete's in Banjermasin in Borneo. I know because I recognised him when I went to the bungalow this morning, and I am perfectly certain that George Marsden Plummer would recognise him, too. With his knowledge Plummer could easily bring the Jap to his will, and therefore what Soto did was in furtherance of Plummer's plan not to help Sonia Vensky, although he allowed her to think so. Dr. Thornton will tell you that 'seroin' is a rare drug produced in Japan and China. I cannot tell you whether Soto had some or whether Plummer provided it, but I am positive it was introduced into the carafe of brandy by the Jap, and into Mr. Constant's system through the medium of the brandy.

"Then, just as Mr. Constant maintains, he became muzzy. It is quite possible that Posani made an attempt to create a quarrel, but before he could do so his vis-a-vis would have fallen forward to the table, overcome by the drug. And then while Posani still sat at the table a hand came out from behind the curtains which hang by the french window. It was that hand that held the weapon which was the cause of Posani's death, and the hand was that of George Marsden Plummer. Plummer is a dead shot to my knowledge, and he could drill Posani in any spot he wished from a much greater distance than that.

"Sonia Vensky heard the shot, and I think we shall find that the Jap witnessed it. The woman thought it was Posani shooting Mr. Constant, and would have rushed in, but was restrained by the Jap. He was holding her until the murderer got away. But when the safe was rifled, and Plummer was gone, the Jap allowed her to go in. Instead of finding Mr. Constant dead she saw him lying across the table snoring, and on the floor was Posani's body.

"No weapon was found on Posani, but a pistol was found on the floor beside Mr. Constant's chair. I shall prove that Posani had a weapon when he went there, and that the weapon was the one which was found on the rug with one chamber discharged. With one exception everything went absolutely according to plan, and that exception depended on chance, which favoured the murderer."

"What was that?" asked Morrison tensely.

"It was chance that the calibre of the weapon used by Plummer happened to be the same as that which Posani had brought with him, but, after all, .38 calibre is the most commonly used, forty-five being favoured mostly by ex-Service men and thirty-two by women. There is a skeleton outline of the case I have to present, Mr. Morrison. And now, again I ask you if you will issue warrants for the immediate arrest of Madame Vali Mata-Vali and her companion who goes under the name of Machado?"

"I—I can do no other," replied Morrison slowly. "I cannot ignore the strong case you make, Mr. Blake. But are you sure you can prove it?"

"Will you accept the evidence of Sonia Vensky?"

"Yes."

"She has made a full confession to me to-night, and will dictate it tomorrow. She knows it is the only way to save herself. And would you accept the evidence of the Jap?"

"He seems one of the most important links."

"He is; and he is in our possession, so to say. At the present moment he is upstairs, where Dr. Thornton has just been setting numerous fractures which he received in a little play of ju-jutsu with my assistant. But I know how to make that little yellow man talk. I know of my own seeing that he was trying to escape to-night to the yacht, Thetis, which anchored off the bungalow to-day. I think the authorities are in danger of finding they have made a mistake in permitting that craft to leave San Diego; but that is no affair of mine. What does concern me is the proof from what I saw that Soto was trying to get to the yacht, and he would only do that if he were in Plummer's service, and the latter knew he must be got away.

"Soto is too important a witness. And for those reasons I believe time to be very limited. I should not be surprised if, even while we talk, George Marsden Plummer and Vali Mata-Vali are not racing for safety. That yacht is only twelve miles distant, if she has not moved even nearer during the last hour or so; and the Mexican border is an easy run from here."

Blake broke off, and Morrison jumped to his feet.

"By thunder, I'm going to get through to headquarters right now!"

19. Police Chase.

WHILE Sexton Blake was elucidating the case as it appeared to him, two of those who were the objects of his remarks were seated in a small room just under the roof of the bungalow, which, for the time being, housed George Marsden Plummer and Vali Mata-Vali.

Seated at a table on which was the complete equipment of a wireless sending and receiving outfit—a portable one, which had been brought from the yacht —Plummer had the headphones over his ears while his finger hovered over the sending-key. For some ten minutes or so he had been in direct communication with the yacht, Thetis, and as, with his free hand, he wrote down the message which was coming through, he ripped out a savage curse.

Vali Mata-Vali was seated close to him, watching the play of expression in his eyes and on his features. She could see that things were bad in some way, but she was too wise to ask questions until Plummer should finish. At last he tore off the earphones and turned to her. For a moment he forgot the sudden crisis of their affairs in contemplation of the extraordinary beauty of the woman who had come into his life at such an opportune moment in Morocco. In that moment Plummer was thinking: "After all, she is a pearl among women; as long as she sticks we can swallow anything, and there are always opportunities to be made."

For George Marsden Plummer knew now that things had come down with a crash in this new plot which they had evolved and carried out with such care. And he knew the cause.

"There is the dickens to pay, Vali," he said, as her eyes sought his. "It is Sexton Blake, I am certain."

"What is it?" she asked, her low tones perfectly level, and her hand quite steady as she flicked the ash from her cigarette. "We have known since this morning that things had become complicated with him taking a hand. He was bound to be dangerous after that Paris affair when he knew I was here."

"And it wouldn't take him long to identify me with Machado," snarled Plummer. "But we've got to make a quick getaway, Vali. I have got the latest from the captain of the Thetis. The Jap has vanished, and the two men he sent ashore to get him have vanished as well. He has sent a party ashore, and they have searched the bungalow. There are signs in the kitchen of a disturbance, but no one there."

"And the Jap's luggage?" she asked quickly.

"Gone!"

"Do you think he has double-crossed us?"

"He wouldn't dare. I tell you, Vali, this is Sexton Blake's work. Besides, the captain got the searchlight to work, and found the boat drifting down the coast. The oars were there, but the two men he sent ashore first have completely vanished."

"Then there is something at work, as you say, mon vieux. I think we had better do as you suggest."

"And there isn't much time."

She smiled, but there was no mirth in that smite,

"It is a pity," she went on, in a conversational tone. "It was such an excellent plot, and those millions, mon vieux, would have come in most useful. But we have a considerable amount of money left, and what is mine is thine. I should have liked to see how the Vensky woman wriggled out of this difficulty."

Plummer looked deep, deep into her eyes.

"You are a wonder, Vali," he said thickly. "Come. Everything is ready, and we shall make for the Mexican border. I have told the captain to stand off outside the three-mile limit and cruise up and down just south of Tia Juana."

Ten minutes later a red rocket tore down the drive of that bungalow. The big, iron gates were already open, for they were worked by an electric button in the garage. The silent swinging back of those gates had caused mild curiosity on the part of a bored plainclothes man, who was keeping a desultory vigil outside. He had moved in, and was peering up the drive, wondering what was up when that rocket appeared.

It swept on like a flash, and before he could spring entirely clear it had struck him, throwing him some twenty feet to one side. Then the great racing car swung at a dangerous angle, and roared off through the night southwards.

Scarcely had it disappeared than a fleet of a dozen police cars came speeding to the bungalow from three different directions. The bruised plainclothes man told a wild story of something that had come upon him like a thunderbolt, and, as he listened to it, Morrison swore softly. He sent three men into the bungalow, but he knew full well that his birds had flown. And then the rest of the fleet went roaring off along the wide, beautifully paved coast road in pursuit of the fugitives.

From the top of a hill as they approached they could see a long stretch of the sea, but now there was not a trace of a riding-light near the shore. All they could glimpse was the sweep of a searchlight far out at sea—well beyond the three-mile limit, they knew.

Not a sign of the big red car they were pursuing. No sign of a rear light ahead of them at all. Easily to be explained that, of course, by the presumption that the fugitives would be travelling without a rear light at all events, in order to hinder pursuit.

But not a sound of anything ahead either. And this was stranger, because however much the fugitives' car might have been subdued by mechanical silencers, some sound of it must have come back in the wake of it through that still night. Yet, though by Morrison's orders the police chasers pulled up with shut-off engines two or three times to listen, not a single betraying sound drifted back to them along that long, long coast road.

And why? Not because as Morrison naturally supposed, the fugitives had got too far ahead. Another and a very different reason was the true one.

This presently became apparent when the leading police car quite suddenly came to a halt and the indicator shot out to pull the whole procession up. Morrison in the second car immediately leapt out and rushed forward to where two of his subordinates (who had jumped from the leading car) were stooping to examine the road with their torches.

"What is it, boys?" he demanded.

"Birds have changed their flight, guv'nor. See here?" returned the senior "boy," and pointed to the road.

Morrison looked, his own torch sweeping down. At once he saw to what the man was pointing. A curved trail of tyre-marks turning left, away from the paved coast road, and continuing along another road through a break in the foothills. A very different road this. Not paved, not even hard as to surface, not made for motoring at all. Just a narrow, rough track, all crumbling and rutty, made for cattle and horse-traffic long years ago before mechanical transport was dreamt of.

"Gee!" exclaimed Morrison in genuine surprise. "They can't have gone that way."

"They have though," answered one of his men, who had run forward along the rough road and now came hurrying back. "The tyre-marks show clear all along. They've gone that way right enough."

"But why? It leads nowhere except among the mountains. Why should they go that way? It don't make sense. Still, if the tyre-marks show— I must see."

He advanced some hundred yards along the rough upland track, and saw. Without any sort of doubt the fugitive car had turned aside and gone that way. The evidence of Morrison's own eyes proved that, and it mystified him more than a bit.

A minute's hard thinking and he was hurrying back to the coast road where the whole fleet of cars had halted.

"See here, boys," he addressed the whole wondering crowd who had quit their several cars and grouped themselves to discuss the unexpected development. "They've gone that way all right. Dunno why they've done it. Seems almost as if this Marsden Plummer's got skeered and gone crazy. Same time we're not bankin' on his havin' turned into a nit-wit. Mebbe he feared we might overrun him before he could make whatever spot he's fixed for a boat to wait for him."

"Most like you're right, sir," struck in another officer. "Belike he's spun a spider-web. Looks like it from the clearness of that left-hand swerve. It's a try-on. Hopes he'll draw the lot of us into this mountain track and get us wedged, it being too narrow to turn except here and there."

Morrison curled his lip in contempt at the suggestion.

"You're a sparkling genius, Murphy," he said scornfully. "But take my tip, my lad, if you're out for promotion don't try it that way. If you're out for the boob prize at an asylum brain-wave contest, all right. Another effort like the one you've jest chucked out, will get ye a walk-over."

"Sorry," muttered Murphy, a bit abashed. "But yer a bit harsh, ain't ye?"

"What?" exploded Morrison. "Still stickin' to wot you said as a real product of genuine grey-matter. Chuck your brains into a sieve my lad, and give 'em a roust-round after adding a little oil. They've gone rusty. Think back about that spider-web spill-out, and ask yourself how Plummer's going to get away with it. How can he turn if we can't? What's more, he can't do with that big car of his what we can, at a pinch, with one of our small buses. He can't go on right through the range. I ain't too familiar with the lay-out of these mountains, but I do know they ain't yet built a racin' track among 'em."

"That's so," confirmed Pesket, another officer. "If Plummer's idea is to go right through, he'll find himself snookered. Only way back to the main coast road is through a gap in the range, and then along a track on the side of the mountains. Full of chasms and man-traps that track is. But even apart from that he'd never be able to make it in a big bus such as he's drivin'."

"There we are then," Morrison said, with his mind made up. "Our plan's clear. Two of you will take the smallest car of the bunch and follow that track through. Two of you in addition to the driver. That's given you three guns to two if you make a round-up and it comes to a shootin' match. You, Peskett, will see to that job, as you know the ground."

"Do the rest of us wait here, sir, for a possible retreat by Plummer on foot? He might abandon the car and try to pad it with the dame he's got with him."

"Not very likely, still he might," Morrison said. "That means some of us will hang on here, while the rest will go on to cut him off, supposing he tries that knife-edge track Peskett spoke of. Everybody back to the cars and get on with the job."

* * * * *

Since it was beyond all doubt that Plummer had turned off the main road and taken to that rough track leading to the perilous mountains, what did it mean?

Simply this: Something had gone wrong with the works!

Speeding along with Plummer at the wheel, and the beautiful Vali Mata-Vali seated beside him, the big red car had made very fast going for a few miles. Then something quite unexpected had happened.

The only warning was a sudden change in the note of the powerful engine. What had been a beautifully even throb subdued by speed to a catlike purr, was abruptly changed into an unexplained and unexplainable clup-clup noise, alternating with a slight metallic jingle.

The first sound of it hit Plummer like a bullet. He pulled up as abruptly as if he had actually been shot.

"What is it?" asked the beautiful woman by his side.

"Don't know," Plummer answered, forcing a calmness he didn't feel so as not to alarm the woman he loved. "Something gone wrong with the car's innards. Don't worry, my dear. I'll soon put it to rights."

But he didn't. You can't put a thing to rights till you know what is wrong. Plummer couldn't find out what was wrong despite his expert knowledge of cars and great mechanical ability. With more time at his disposal he probably would have discovered the fault, but more time was just the thing he couldn't afford to spend over it.

Even in his brief examination, he twice broke off to listen hard with his eyes directed back along the road they had come. The woman could read him like a book, and instantly divined what was in his mind.

"You are what you call it—ha, stumped?" she said lightly and with a ravishing smile despite her own anxiety.

"You've hit it, my dear. I am stumped. Can't see what's wrong with the blamed machine."

"And you can't spare enough time over it to find out. You fear our pursuers may overtake us, n'est ce pas?"

"Right again, honey. The cursed cops are after us by now and they've got pretty slick machines. We mustn't wait about any longer. So long as this car was all right we were safe. We could have shown them a clean pair of heels. But now—" Plummer broke off with a shrug and a deep frown.

"What, then, do we do?" she asked. "We can't stay here."

"No, ma cherie, we are not going to stay here!" His smile was sardonic.

"But if you think the car will break down—"

"As I fear it will before long," Plummer broke in. "We've got to beat the swine somehow, and since we can't do it by speed we must do it by cunning."

"Ha! What—"

"Game for a gamble, honey?"

"Mais oui, with you, George. Anything with you.—What—what is your gamble this time?"

He waved his hand to the left as he again got into the driving seat.

"We make for the mountains. It's dangerous, but not so dangerous as keeping to this road with the car as it is. You'll chance it?"

"Parbleu—yes!" She turned her eyes on him. "Anywhere with you."

"Then on we go. A bit on there is a track leading to the left. If the bus doesn't conk out before we get there, we'll be all right."

"But if not?"

"We'll find some other way out." he answered. "However the game may go at first, we'll win in the end. Damn the thing!"

For no sooner had he started than again there came that strange clup-clup sound and the indeterminate jingle of metal as if some obscure steel part were loose in the hidden mechanism.

But they went forward all right, though at a greatly reduced speed. Plummer, in fact, was afraid to travel very fast lest something should snap and bring about calamity. The track to the left of which he had spoken, was about a third of a mile on, and fervently he prayed to the Devil that the car would, at any rate, carry them safely that far.

The Devil has a well established reputation for looking after his own, and answered Plummer's prayer. With the road still clear—no sign or sound of their pursuers as he looked back— they reached the point where the track ran out of it, ran upward through the foothills, and so away to the loftier mountains.

He turned the big car. Very slowly of necessity, and it was that which made the deep impress which the police were afterwards to notice.

Even as he made those deep impressions, it came to Plummer that the pursuing police would spot them. Well, it couldn't be helped. If they did, they would doubtless send part of their force along that mountain track in an attempt to over-run him.

Vali Mata-Vali thought of that, too, and mentioned it, not fearfully, but still with a smile. Plummer smiled back as they started along the rough, ascending track, and answered with the sudden idea which had come to him.

"You are right, ma cherie. They'll no doubt see our tyre marks and follow us this way. Well, let them. Let us but get really among the mountains a mile or so on, and they'll never find us."

"What do you mean, George? This car is big. We cannot park it out of sight. There is no room on this narrow way."

Plummer's eyes were alight as with flame.

"We are going to get rid of the car, my dear. It's no use hanging on to it damaged as it is. If it'll only carry us to where I mean, over it goes!"

"Over where?"

"The gorge, honey. A mile on, there is a gap in this track. It opens on to a split in the mountains. A deep chasm. We're going to pitch the car over that so that the police, when they come, will see!"

"And think it was an accident? You mean they'll think you and I have gone over with it in the dark?"

"That's it. They'll stop the pursuit and descend the ravine to search for us."

"And we? We hurry on foot, do you mean?"

"No, my dear. Too slow and too far. We hide up. Plenty of caves and cubby-holes where they'd never find us in a month of Sundays. We hide up till they arrive, and watch them start on their search of the ravine."

"And then?"

"It will depend on how things work out. We trust to luck. Now, if only this car will carry us so far! She's getting terribly wonky, but with luck we shall manage it."

The luck held. Labouring hard like a corpulent man with asthma, the big car moved slowly up and up the mountain path, until Plummer brought it to a halt near to the place he wanted.

Right in their way was a hummock of scrub-clad rock which to avoid would have required a sudden turn to the half-left, had their purpose been to follow along the track they had been pursuing. But since their purpose was not that, Plummer had brought the car to a halt without any turn at all. Where he had stopped it, it faced an opening to the right of the high, jutting rock, and where the land on that side fell away with a suddenness that would have appalled anybody unacquainted with the place.

And not only appalled, but have brought a careless motorist to sudden and certain death!

For that opening formed the lip of a ghastly chasm fully four hundred feet deep. Its bed was a split in the mountain—a ravine, steep again in its turn, down which tumbled a mountain stream that fell over its rugged bed towards the flat ground still much farther below.

"Here we are!" muttered Plummer, as they alighted. "Here's the place I spoke of. Careful now, ma cherie. Not too close to the edge! Take my hand!"

For Vali had advanced quite close to the edge of the abyss, trying to pierce the depths in the darkness of the night.

"What a place!" she murmured, with a shudder. "And you are going to pitch the car over there?"

"That's the idea."

She shuddered again.

"We might have gone over with it had you not known the place and slowed up."

Plummer grinned.

"Easily. That's why I chose the spot. If the police follow us this way, that's just what they'll think. That we have gone over. But now to work. First, we must take certain things from the locker likely to be useful to us. Then over the edge the car will go! To work, honey—to work!"

20.   At the "Devil's Leap."

TOILING up that steep, rough track along which Plummer and his fair companion had come, was another car. One of the smaller of the several police cars which had set out in their pursuit.

At the wheel sat the police driver— one Haswell—a smallish, lean man wearing a leather overall and a cap with projecting peak. Beside him sat Peskett, the officer whom Morrison had selected for the job on account of his knowledge of the mountain track. Another officer, a big, brawny fellow named Groby, sat behind.

That they were going right, that the fugitive car had really gone right on— and not merely entered the hilly road and then backed in its own tracks as a blind, as some of the police had been inclined to suspect—was the more perceptible the farther they went.

Halting now and then to examine the ground, they found every time the deep indentations which the big car had made in the soft, unmade-up track, and they knew that the fugitives were to be sought somewhere ahead of them amid those mountain fastnesses.

Watching the trail keenly, Peskett sat with puckered brows speculating on what the upshot of this adventure was likely to be.

"They'll never get that big bus of theirs along the mountain side," he muttered to Haswell "We could manage it with this one—though that would need careful driving—but with a big affair like theirs, well"—he shrugged his broad shoulders—"it would be impossible— quite impossible. It would mean death to venture."

"Then what'll they do?"

"Guess when they see what they're up against, they'll shut off steam and quit their car."

"And then what? Pad it?"

"It'll be their only way."

"That case we're bound to overtake 'em."

"Sure thing. But if they hear us coming they'll try to hide up, so we'll have to keep our eyes skinned."

"Come to that," Peskitt added a minute later, "we've gotta keep our peepers peeled now. We're gettin' near to the 'Devil's Leap'."

"What the devil's that?"

"A break in the mountain side. A chasm jest about as deep as hell. Look out for a big rock juttin' out ahead of us. The track wheels round to the left of it, but I'll give you the tip when we get near to it.
126

I've been this way a time or two before."

On for another half-mile or so, then: "Slow up!" exclaimed Peskitt. "That black lump ahead is the rock I spoke of. Keep well to the near side. The ground slopes away nastily, so keep well away to the left if you don't want to go post-haste to hell before your time!"

Going slowly, Haswell kept the police car close under the mountain wall on the left-hand side. Suddenly, as they drew within a few yards of the projecting rock, Peskitt hissed out excitedly:

"Stop!"

Haswell stopped. More excited than ever, Peskitt leapt out, Groby following him. Cautiously, Peskitt moved forward a few yards, then, dropping to his knees, flashed his torch.

"Gosh!" he gasped, pointing to the ground. "They've gone over! Look!"

No doubt about it. Deep tyre marks in the ground proved beyond dispute that the big car had gone down that patch of sloping ground, right over the edge, then down,—down to death and destruction in that deep abyss.

"Gone, both of 'em!" panted Peskett, peering over the edge. "Not the first to 'a' missed the turn in the dark."

"Not a doubt of that," assented his companion. "Waal, I guess they've cheated the chair. Jest as well p'r'aps for them, for they'd have sure been for the hot-plate. Wot do we do about it, Pesky?"

"We've got to get 'em," responded Peskett, mopping moisture from his brow. "We missed 'em alive, but we've got to take 'em dead!"

"But they'll sure be in bits or smashed to a pulp!"

"Then we've gotta pick up the pieces and take 'em along to the chief like that."

"But how do we get along down there?"

"This way. Foller me. I know a path. We'll tell Haswell, and then get on with the grisly business."

Three minutes later they had started. They took their guns with them, not that they were likely to need those. Also their torches, with spare bulbs. These they were likely to need, for the way down into that abyss was long and dangerous. Black as a well of ink, too, and likely to take a long time to reach the bottom.

As they began the descent, Haswell lay face downward with his eyes over the brink and his torch in his hand. He watched them for a minute or two till the contour of the rocky cliff-face hid them from his view.

Then he scrambled to his feet, walked a few yards out of the wind, and, sitting down with his back to a rock, lit a cigar.

Meditatively he smoked. He guessed he had a long time to kill. It would take Peskett and Groby an hour at least to do their grisly job, and it might even take several. He smoked on, resigned to patience.

Pity he hadn't taken more trouble about the selection of his resting-place. His back was to a rock, it is true. But just to the right of him was a split in the rock. A crevice wide enough for an enemy to creep through and attack him from behind. But if such a thought as that had come to Haswell at all—and it didn't, for he wasn't a bit imaginative—he would have laughed it to scorn. Who was likely to be hanging about on a black, cold, mountain path at such a time of night, so where could the enemy come from?

All the same, there were two enemies watching him—as they had watched the whole episode—from a distance of little more than ten yards away. Deadly enemies, too. George Marsden Plummer and Vali the Frenchwoman. And Plummer—as he had already told the woman in a whisper—looked upon the waiting policeman as his lawful—or, rather unlawful—prey.

From the cave in which they had been hiding near by, they stole out. While the woman took up a position behind a huge boulder, the man made for the split in the great mass of rock against which Haswell was sitting. Through the split he stealthily edged himself, drawing foot by foot and then inch by inch nearer to the squatted officer. And there at the back of him, within a mere few inches, he crouched a moment.

Drawing his heavy-butted revolver, he clubbed it in his right hand. Outward and upward stole that same hand. For a split second it hovered just over the side of the unsuspecting officer's head. Then—

Crash! against the man's temple, and Haswell crumpled up sideways without even so much as a moan.

When, some three hours later, Peskett and Groby returned from the depths of the ravine—where they had found the big car smashed to bits, but no sign of the two crooks they had supposed to be in it—it was to discover their comrade Haswell battered and drugged, but still alive, with his legs bound with rope and his wrists secured by his own handcuffs, which Plummer had taken from his pocket.

But of the resourceful Plummer himself and his woman companion, nothing was to be seen by them, or any of their comrades waiting elsewhere for that matter. Nor of their own car, which they had left in charge of Haswell.

For Plummer and Vali Mata-Vali had made off in that immediately after placing Haswell hors de combat. And in it they had safely reached a point on the coast from which they had been able to signal their yacht in Morse by means of a powerful lamp Plummer had carried with him for that purpose.

They had followed that knife-edge track along the mountain—of which Peskett had spoken—for some distance, but not all the way. For Plummer, anticipating that more police would be watching the junction of that with the main road, turned off by another rough track which had its exit from the mountain district farther south. He was thus able to strike the coast road some miles farther along, and so completely avoid the quite inadequate net which Morrison had spread for him.

Then, after making sure that a boat was coming for him in response to his Morse signals, Plummer abandoned the car amid a grove of trees. It was found there some hours later by some of the police searchers. In it was an open sheet of paper with an ironic message written by Plummer, addressed jointly to Morrison and Sexton Blake.

It told briefly what had happened amid the mountains, apologised mockingly for having to put Haswell out in order to borrow the car, inquired caustically after their healths, and at the same time assured them that he himself and his companion were quite well, thank you! Out and out ruffian that he was, capable of any evil thing from murder downwards, George Marsden Plummer had within him a streak of sardonic humour which he loved to indulge on occasions.

It was a very sore Morrison that returned to Hollywood that night, or, rather, morning.

But the final bitter pill came when the police analyst issued his report of his test of the inside of the carafe that had held the brandy at the bungalow. He found slight traces of something which he was able to identify as the rare drug, seroin.

Needless to say, the formal appearance of Peter J. Constant at the interrogation which followed—it could not be called a trial—was one of the sensations of the year. Sexton Blake went into the stand and marshaled his facts, one by one, in such a way that it all seemed ridiculously clear.

Sonia Vensky's statement was read in full, and an even greater sensation was caused. But the "piece de resistance," as it were, was the production of the Japanese houseboy, who, under the "gentle" methods of persuasion used by the American police, came out with a full confession.

The real triumph of Sexton Blake's methods was shown when a court was told that, in the lacquered box which Soto had been about to take with him in the flight, were the twelve million odd in bearer bonds and cash which Peter J. Constant had placed in the safe at the bungalow in preparation for his own flight. It was the last thread of proof that completed the fabric which the great British detective had woven out of mere bits of scattered clues, and it completed his case which charged Vali Mata-Vali and George Marsden Plummer, alias Jorge Machado, with having instigated and carried out the killing of Paolo Posani, showing at the same time how Plummer had bent the Jap completely to his own purpose. It seemed all too plain, as Blake explained things, that, after the killing, the safe had been rifled by Plummer, but that he had feared, in case of suspicion the yacht might be searched, or else he dared not trust them in care of the captain. Nor would he be able to take the risk of keeping them in the bungalow he and Vali Mata-Vali were occupying at Hollywood. Where could he find a safer guardian than Soto, who was now his creature and depended upon him for his every breath of freedom? And when he should give the Jap the word to flee from the bungalow to the yacht, what easier than for him to take the bonds with him? Thus had Plummer figured, and would have succeeded in his plans but for Sexton Blake.

Blake's statement of the case was clinched by the production of the two Tangerines who had come ashore from the yacht.

The only criticism made of Blake was that he had used somewhat highhanded methods, but here Morrison stepped into the limelight by announcing publicly that Mr. Blake had been quite justified in using those methods in his efforts to clear an innocent man.

Thus closed the sensational Constant Bungalow Affair; or, as it was called by some, the Hollywood Scandal, but Hollywood has so many scandals that the former served to identify it better.

As for Sonia Vensky, her statement enabled her to avoid any prosecution. But a few weeks later she figured again in the public eye, when Peter J. Constant divorced her. He was extremely generous in the matter, settling a million dollars on her, and with this she departed for parts unknown. The Japanese houseboy was deported.

But the most irritating bit of news that reached Morrison was some weeks later, when the report came through that the famous French actress, Madame Vali Mata-Vali, was creating a furore in Mexico City in the part of La Dame aux Camellias. And Morrison couldn't do a thing while extradition from Mexico was a dead letter.

Finally, when Sexton Blake and Tinker did get away from Los Angeles they took with them one of the biggest fees that had ever come into the coffers at Baker Street. Peter J. Constant was a grateful man, and to-day he is a very much wiser one.

THE END.

www.ingramcontent.com/pod-product-compliance
Lightning Source LLC
Chambersburg PA
CBHW050825180626
46814CB00004B/1465